W9-AWQ-104

William Shakespeare's
Julius Caesar

adapted by **Vincent Goodwin**
illustrated by **Fred Perry**

visit us at
www.abdopublishing.com

Published by Magic Wagon, a division of the ABDO Group, 8000 West 78th Street, Edina, Minnesota, 55439. Copyright © 2011 by Abdo Consulting Group, Inc. International copyrights reserved in all countries. All rights reserved. No part of this book may be reproduced in any form without written permission from the publisher.

Graphic Planet™ is a trademark and logo of Magic Wagon.

Printed in the United States of America, North Mankato, Minnesota.
052010
092010

J-GN
GRAPHIC PLANET
399-3659

Adapted by Vincent Goodwin
Illustrated by Fred Perry
Edited by Stephanie Hedlund and Rochelle Baltzer
Interior layout and design by Antarctic Press
Cover art by Fred Perry
Cover design by Abbey Fitzgerald

Library of Congress Cataloging-in-Publication Data

Goodwin, Vincent.
 William Shakespeare's Julius Caesar / adapted by Vincent Goodwin ; illustrated by Fred Perry.
   p. cm. -- (Graphic Shakespeare)
 Summary: Retells, in comic book format, Shakespeare's play about political intrigue, personal betrayal, and the aftermath of a brutal assassination.
 ISBN 978-1-60270-765-8
 1. Graphic novels. [1. Graphic novels. 2. Shakespeare, William, 1564-1616. Julius Caesar-- Adaptations.] I. Perry, Fred, 1969- ill. II. Shakespeare, William, 1564-1616. Julius Caesar. III. Title. IV. Title: Julius Caesar.
 PZ7.7.G66Wek 2010
 741.5'973--dc22

                        2010011054

Table of Contents

Cast of Characters

Julius Caesar

Brutus
Conspirator against Julius

Cassius
Conspirator against Julius

Casca
Conspirator against Julius

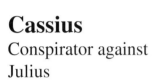

Decius
Conspirator against Julius

Marc Antony
Leader after Julius's death

Octavius Caesar
Leader after Julius's death

Lepidus
Leader after Julius's death

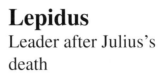

Messala
Friend of Brutus and Cassius

Pindarus
Servant to Cassius

Flavius
Servant to Brutus

Dardanius
Servant to Brutus

Voluminius
Friend of Brutus and Cassius

Julius Caesar is set in ancient Rome around 44 BC. Rome is the capital of Italy. Rome was a republic and democratically ruled by senators during Caesar's lifetime. Rome was probably the strongest nation in that area. Caesar led armies that conquered the surrounding areas. This gained him respect from aristocrats and the poor.

Caesar was one of the only rulers who were sympathetic to the poor. The masses respected him and thought of him as the best ruler in the republic. This was unacceptable to the other senators. So, they decided to get rid of Caesar before he could change Rome into a tyranny.

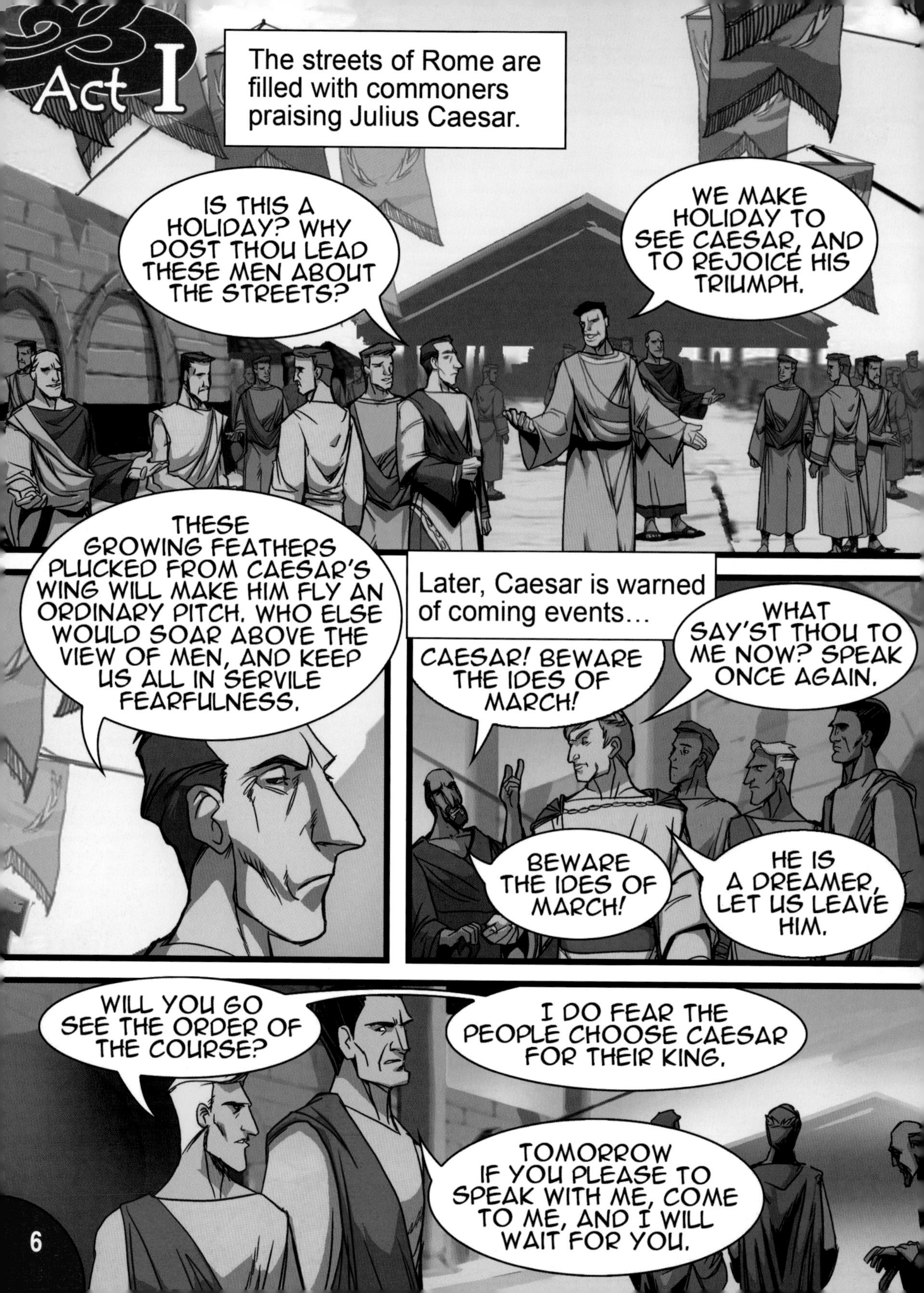
Act I
The streets of Rome are filled with commoners praising Julius Caesar.
IS THIS A HOLIDAY? WHY DOST THOU LEAD THESE MEN ABOUT THE STREETS?
WE MAKE HOLIDAY TO SEE CAESAR, AND TO REJOICE HIS TRIUMPH.
THESE GROWING FEATHERS PLUCKED FROM CAESAR'S WING WILL MAKE HIM FLY AN ORDINARY PITCH. WHO ELSE WOULD SOAR ABOVE THE VIEW OF MEN, AND KEEP US ALL IN SERVILE FEARFULNESS.
Later, Caesar is warned of coming events…
CAESAR! BEWARE THE IDES OF MARCH!
WHAT SAY'ST THOU TO ME NOW? SPEAK ONCE AGAIN.
BEWARE THE IDES OF MARCH!
HE IS A DREAMER, LET US LEAVE HIM.
WILL YOU GO SEE THE ORDER OF THE COURSE?
I DO FEAR THE PEOPLE CHOOSE CAESAR FOR THEIR KING.
TOMORROW IF YOU PLEASE TO SPEAK WITH ME, COME TO ME, AND I WILL WAIT FOR YOU.

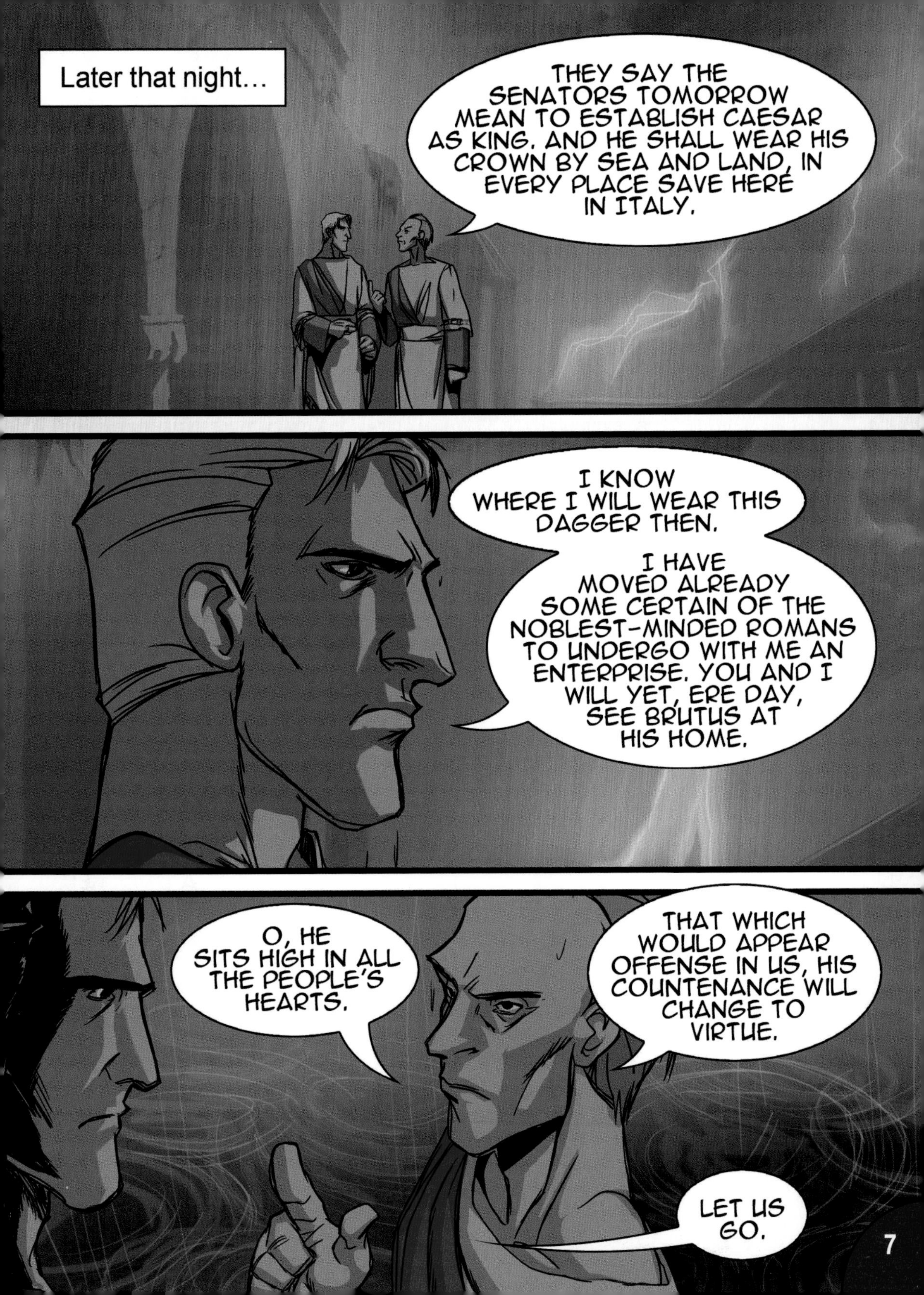
Later that night…
THEY SAY THE SENATORS TOMORROW MEAN TO ESTABLISH CAESAR AS KING. AND HE SHALL WEAR HIS CROWN BY SEA AND LAND, IN EVERY PLACE SAVE HERE IN ITALY.
I KNOW WHERE I WILL WEAR THIS DAGGER THEN.
I HAVE MOVED ALREADY SOME CERTAIN OF THE NOBLEST-MINDED ROMANS TO UNDERGO WITH ME AN ENTERPRISE. YOU AND I WILL YET, ERE DAY, SEE BRUTUS AT HIS HOME.
O, HE SITS HIGH IN ALL THE PEOPLE'S HEARTS.
THAT WHICH WOULD APPEAR OFFENSE IN US, HIS COUNTENANCE WILL CHANGE TO VIRTUE.
LET US GO.

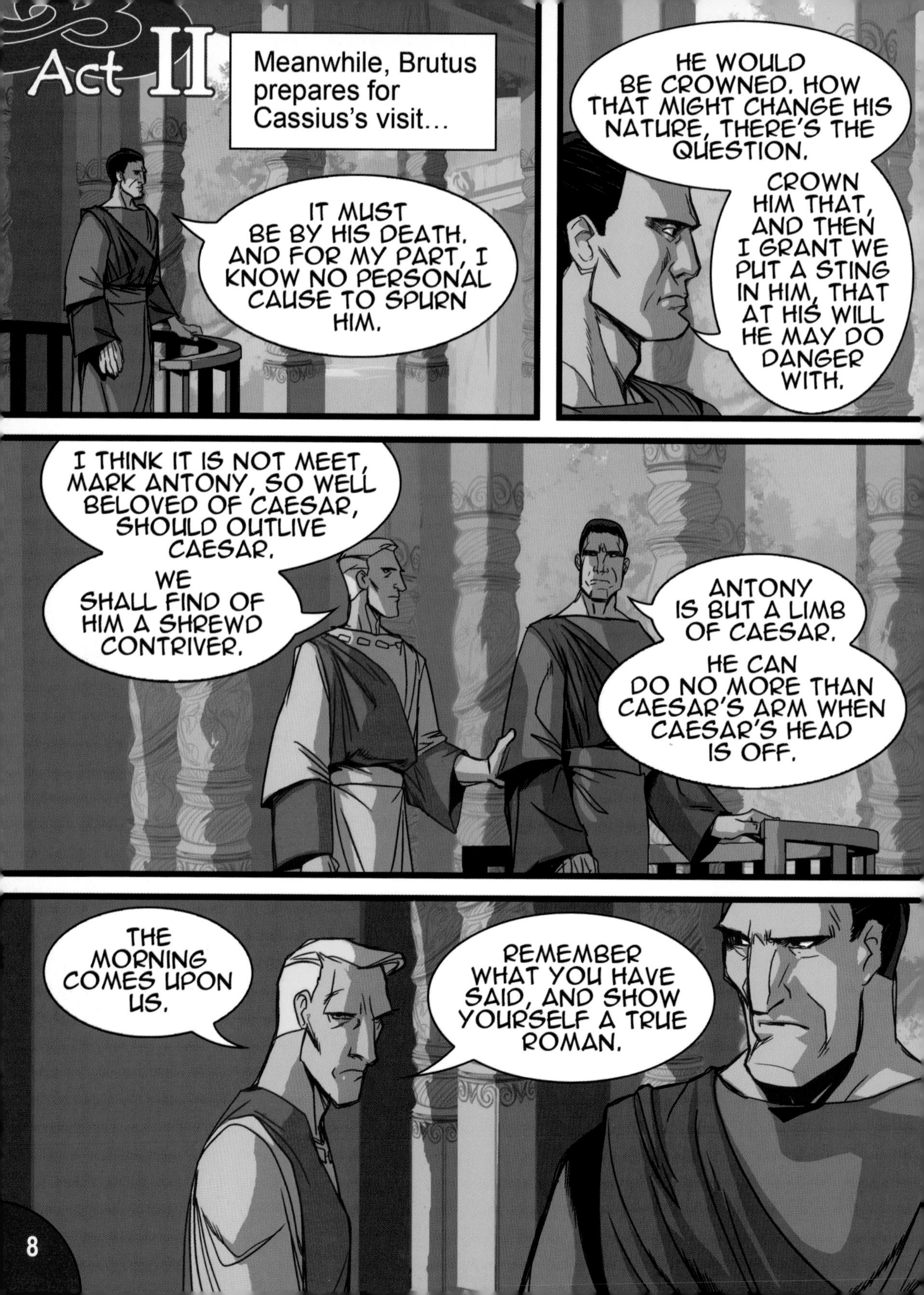
Act II
Meanwhile, Brutus prepares for Cassius's visit…
IT MUST BE BY HIS DEATH. AND FOR MY PART, I KNOW NO PERSONAL CAUSE TO SPURN HIM.
HE WOULD BE CROWNED. HOW THAT MIGHT CHANGE HIS NATURE, THERE'S THE QUESTION.
CROWN HIM THAT, AND THEN I GRANT WE PUT A STING IN HIM, THAT AT HIS WILL HE MAY DO DANGER WITH.
I THINK IT IS NOT MEET, MARK ANTONY, SO WELL BELOVED OF CAESAR, SHOULD OUTLIVE CAESAR.
WE SHALL FIND OF HIM A SHREWD CONTRIVER.
ANTONY IS BUT A LIMB OF CAESAR.
HE CAN DO NO MORE THAN CAESAR'S ARM WHEN CAESAR'S HEAD IS OFF.
THE MORNING COMES UPON US.
REMEMBER WHAT YOU HAVE SAID, AND SHOW YOURSELF A TRUE ROMAN.

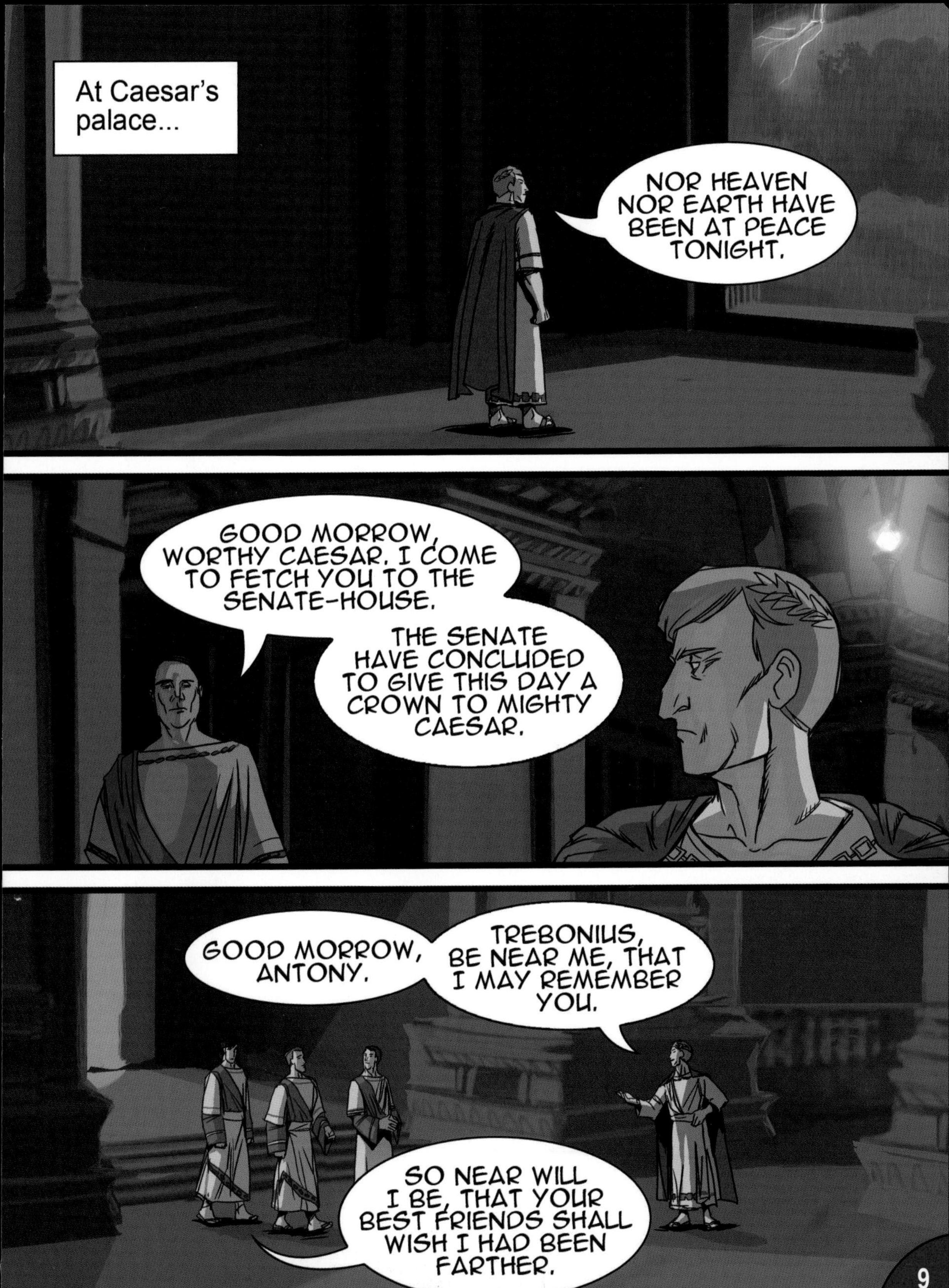
At Caesar's palace...
NOR HEAVEN NOR EARTH HAVE BEEN AT PEACE TONIGHT.
GOOD MORROW, WORTHY CAESAR. I COME TO FETCH YOU TO THE SENATE-HOUSE.
THE SENATE HAVE CONCLUDED TO GIVE THIS DAY A CROWN TO MIGHTY CAESAR.
GOOD MORROW, ANTONY.
TREBONIUS, BE NEAR ME, THAT I MAY REMEMBER YOU.
SO NEAR WILL I BE, THAT YOUR BEST FRIENDS SHALL WISH I HAD BEEN FARTHER.

Act III

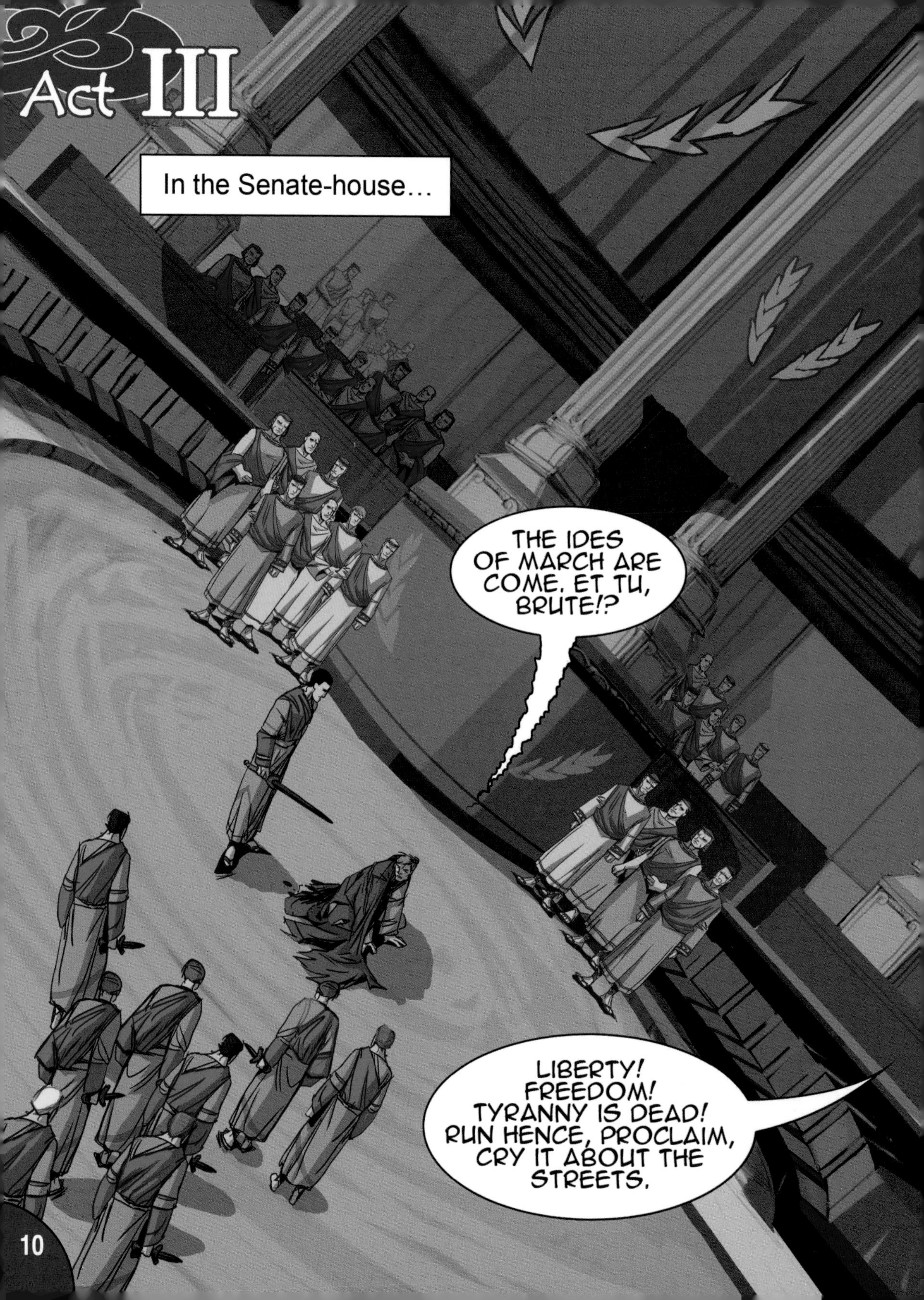
In the Senate-house…
THE IDES OF MARCH ARE COME. ET TU, BRUTE!?
LIBERTY! FREEDOM! TYRANNY IS DEAD! RUN HENCE, PROCLAIM, CRY IT ABOUT THE STREETS.

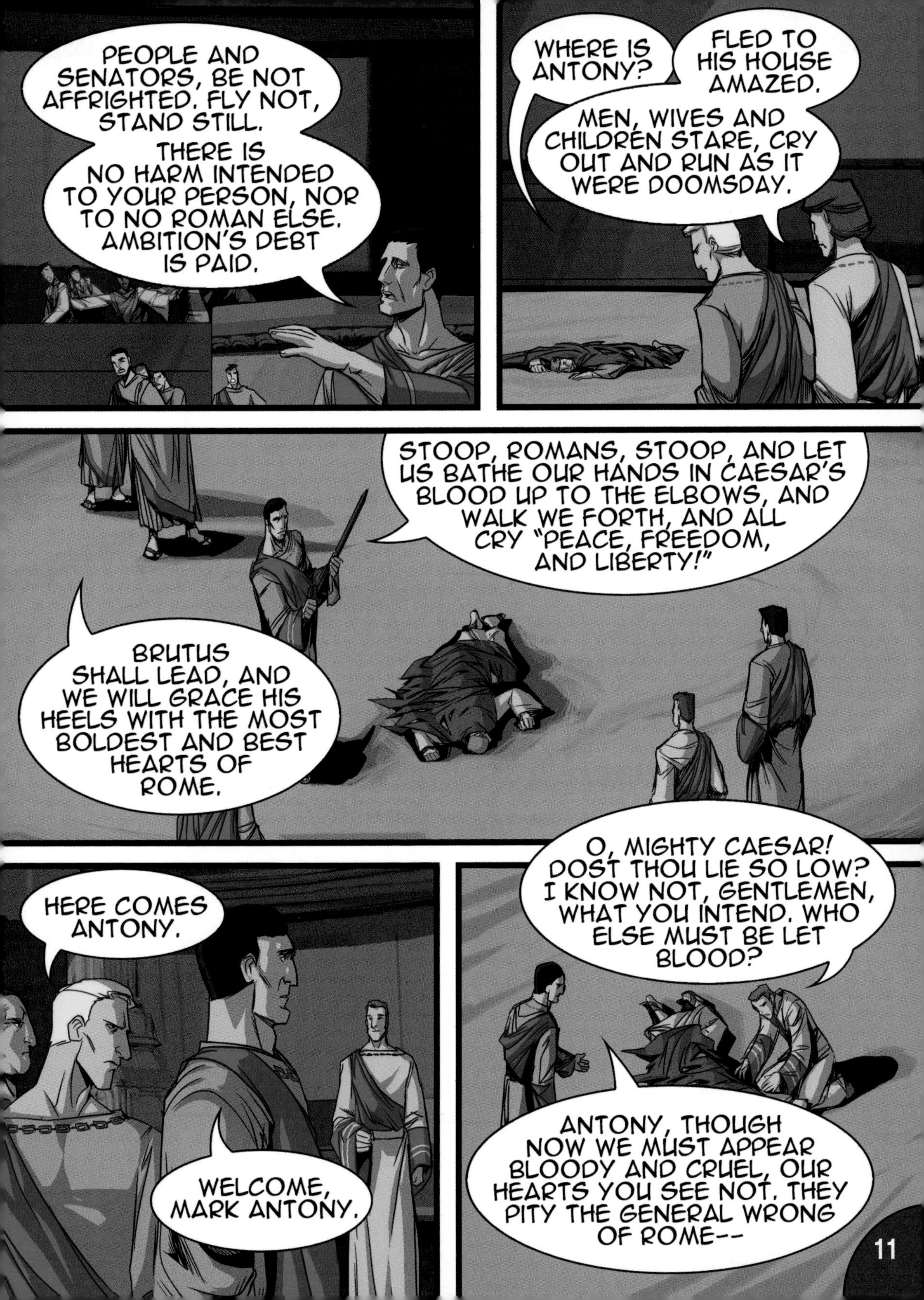
PEOPLE AND SENATORS, BE NOT AFFRIGHTED. FLY NOT, STAND STILL.
THERE IS NO HARM INTENDED TO YOUR PERSON, NOR TO NO ROMAN ELSE. AMBITION'S DEBT IS PAID.
WHERE IS ANTONY?
FLED TO HIS HOUSE AMAZED.
MEN, WIVES AND CHILDREN STARE, CRY OUT AND RUN AS IT WERE DOOMSDAY.
STOOP, ROMANS, STOOP, AND LET US BATHE OUR HANDS IN CAESAR'S BLOOD UP TO THE ELBOWS, AND WALK WE FORTH, AND ALL CRY "PEACE, FREEDOM, AND LIBERTY!"
BRUTUS SHALL LEAD, AND WE WILL GRACE HIS HEELS WITH THE MOST BOLDEST AND BEST HEARTS OF ROME.
HERE COMES ANTONY.
WELCOME, MARK ANTONY.
O, MIGHTY CAESAR! DOST THOU LIE SO LOW? I KNOW NOT, GENTLEMEN, WHAT YOU INTEND. WHO ELSE MUST BE LET BLOOD?
ANTONY, THOUGH NOW WE MUST APPEAR BLOODY AND CRUEL, OUR HEARTS YOU SEE NOT. THEY PITY THE GENERAL WRONG OF ROME--

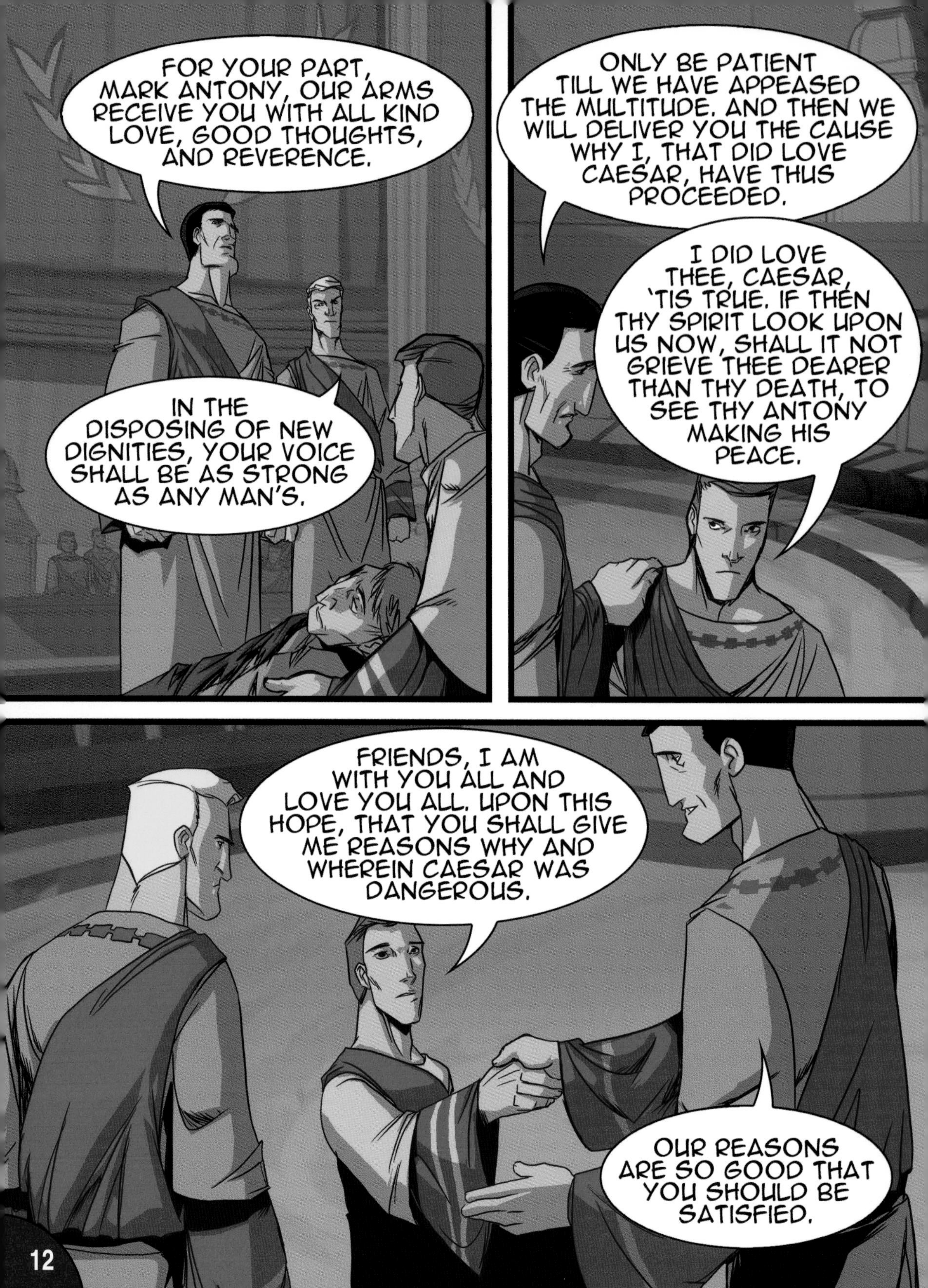
FOR YOUR PART, MARK ANTONY, OUR ARMS RECEIVE YOU WITH ALL KIND LOVE, GOOD THOUGHTS, AND REVERENCE.
IN THE DISPOSING OF NEW DIGNITIES, YOUR VOICE SHALL BE AS STRONG AS ANY MAN'S.
ONLY BE PATIENT TILL WE HAVE APPEASED THE MULTITUDE. AND THEN WE WILL DELIVER YOU THE CAUSE WHY I, THAT DID LOVE CAESAR, HAVE THUS PROCEEDED.
I DID LOVE THEE, CAESAR, 'TIS TRUE. IF THEN THY SPIRIT LOOK UPON US NOW, SHALL IT NOT GRIEVE THEE DEARER THAN THY DEATH, TO SEE THY ANTONY MAKING HIS PEACE.
FRIENDS, I AM WITH YOU ALL AND LOVE YOU ALL. UPON THIS HOPE, THAT YOU SHALL GIVE ME REASONS WHY AND WHEREIN CAESAR WAS DANGEROUS.
OUR REASONS ARE SO GOOD THAT YOU SHOULD BE SATISFIED.

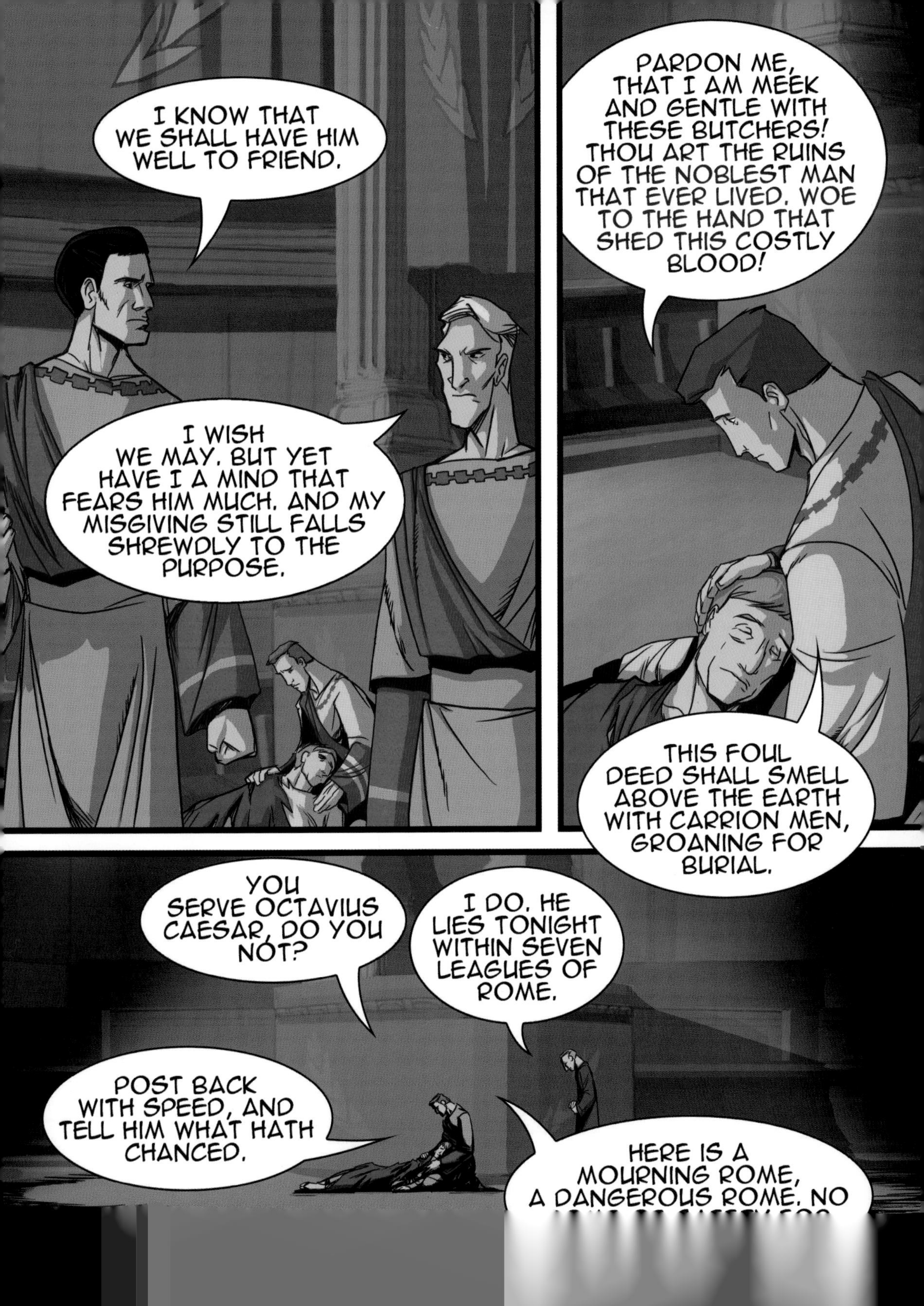
I KNOW THAT WE SHALL HAVE HIM WELL TO FRIEND.
I WISH WE MAY. BUT YET HAVE I A MIND THAT FEARS HIM MUCH. AND MY MISGIVING STILL FALLS SHREWDLY TO THE PURPOSE.
PARDON ME, THAT I AM MEEK AND GENTLE WITH THESE BUTCHERS! THOU ART THE RUINS OF THE NOBLEST MAN THAT EVER LIVED. WOE TO THE HAND THAT SHED THIS COSTLY BLOOD!
THIS FOUL DEED SHALL SMELL ABOVE THE EARTH WITH CARRION MEN, GROANING FOR BURIAL.
YOU SERVE OCTAVIUS CAESAR, DO YOU NOT?
I DO. HE LIES TONIGHT WITHIN SEVEN LEAGUES OF ROME.
POST BACK WITH SPEED, AND TELL HIM WHAT HATH CHANCED.
HERE IS A MOURNING ROME, A DANGEROUS ROME. NO

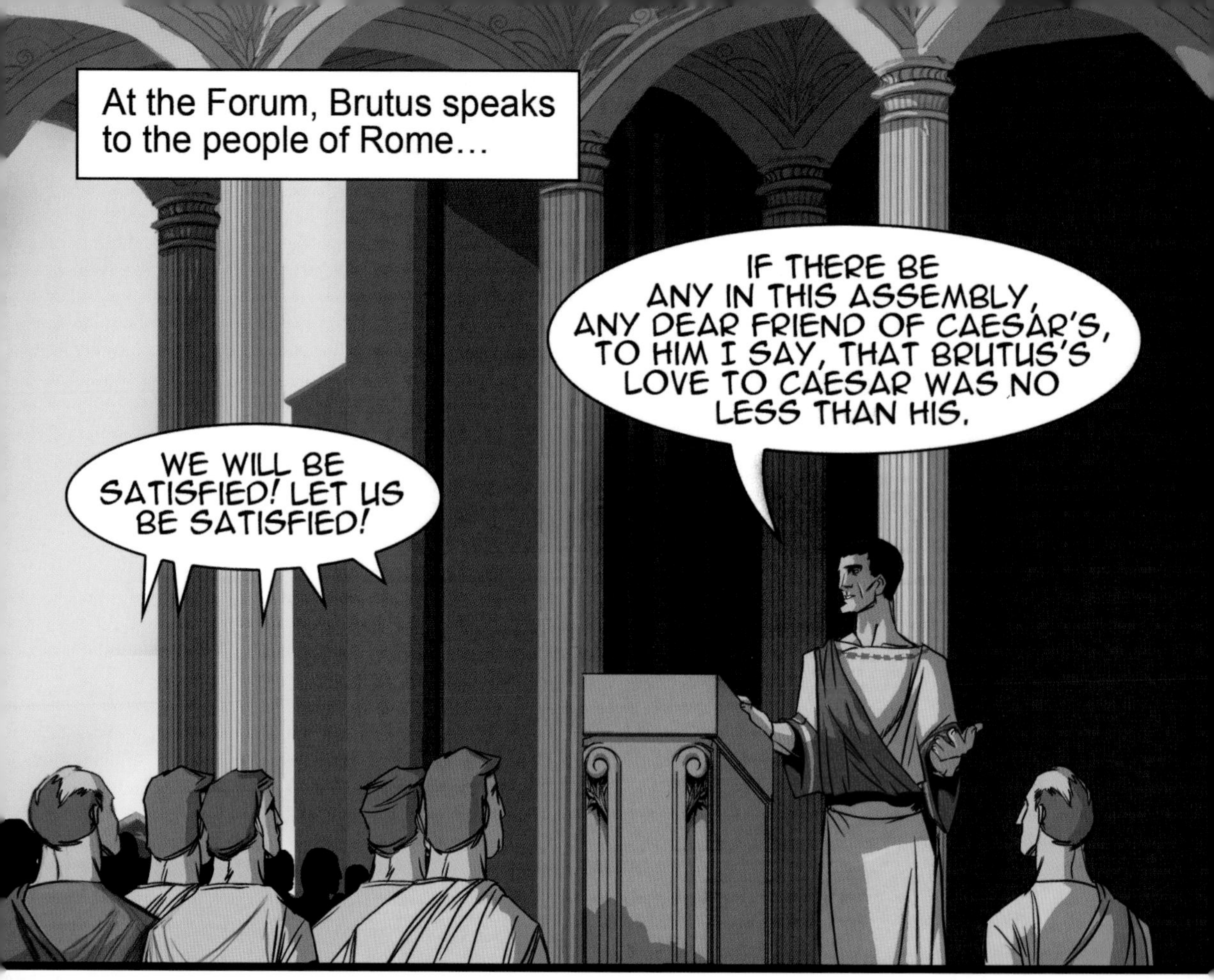
At the Forum, Brutus speaks to the people of Rome…
IF THERE BE ANY IN THIS ASSEMBLY, ANY DEAR FRIEND OF CAESAR'S, TO HIM I SAY, THAT BRUTUS'S LOVE TO CAESAR WAS NO LESS THAN HIS.
WE WILL BE SATISFIED! LET US BE SATISFIED!

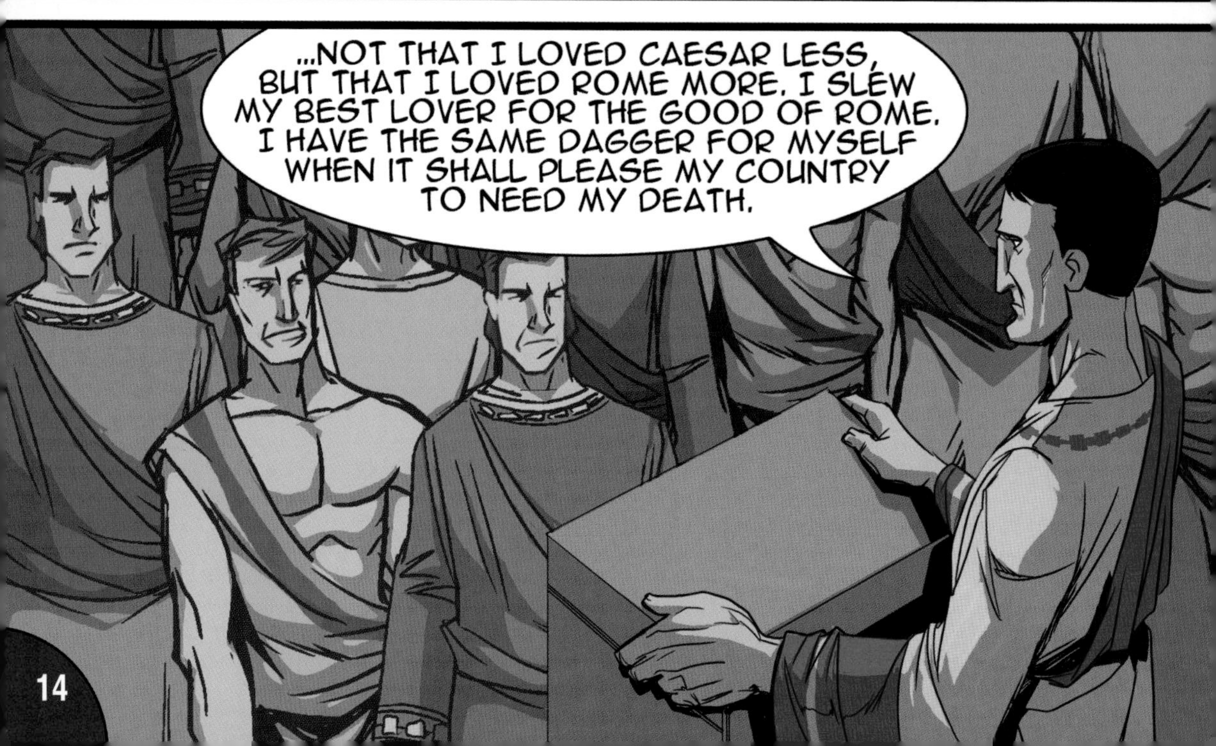
...NOT THAT I LOVED CAESAR LESS, BUT THAT I LOVED ROME MORE. I SLEW MY BEST LOVER FOR THE GOOD OF ROME. I HAVE THE SAME DAGGER FOR MYSELF WHEN IT SHALL PLEASE MY COUNTRY TO NEED MY DEATH.

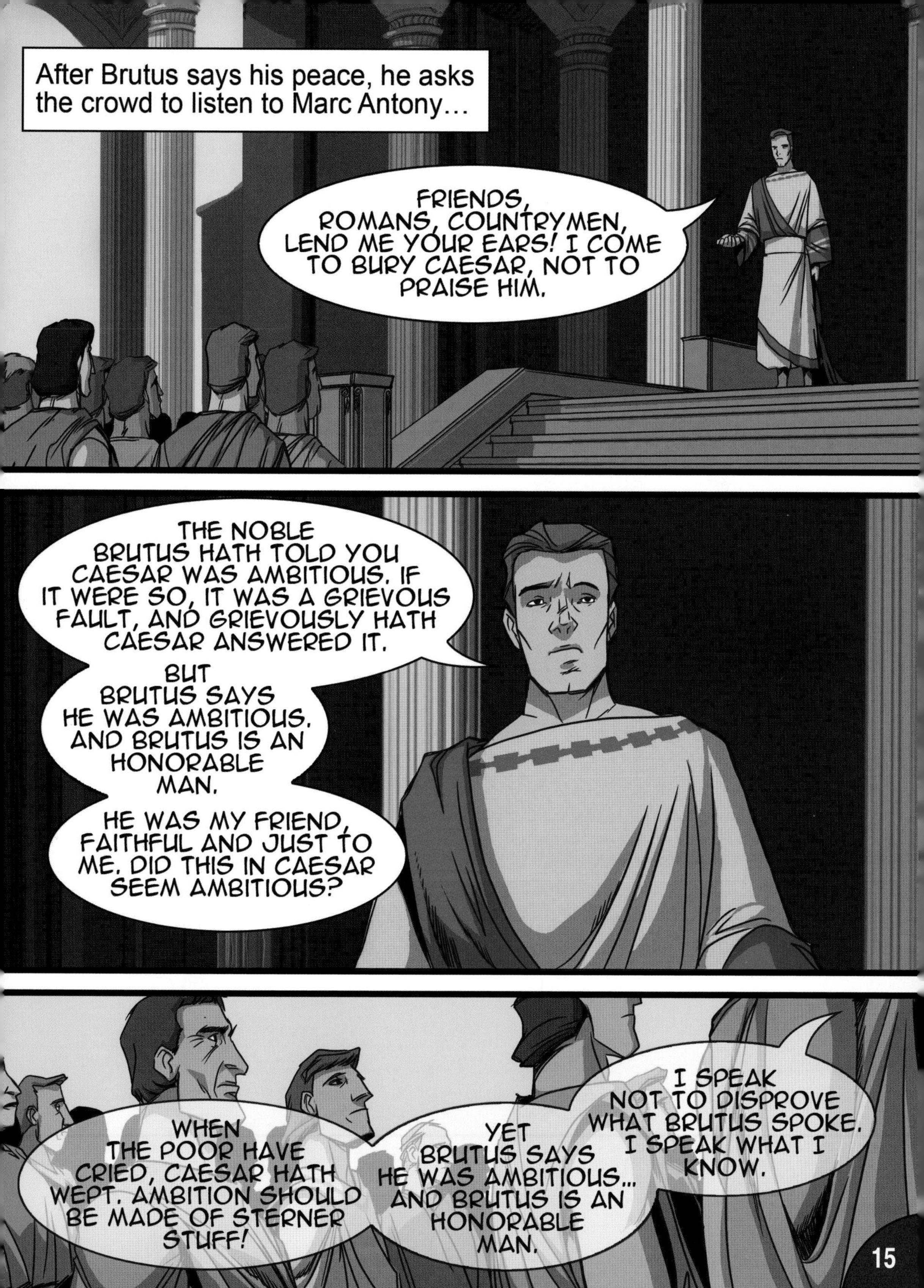
After Brutus says his peace, he asks the crowd to listen to Marc Antony…
FRIENDS, ROMANS, COUNTRYMEN, LEND ME YOUR EARS! I COME TO BURY CAESAR, NOT TO PRAISE HIM.
THE NOBLE BRUTUS HATH TOLD YOU CAESAR WAS AMBITIOUS. IF IT WERE SO, IT WAS A GRIEVOUS FAULT, AND GRIEVOUSLY HATH CAESAR ANSWERED IT.
BUT BRUTUS SAYS HE WAS AMBITIOUS. AND BRUTUS IS AN HONORABLE MAN.
HE WAS MY FRIEND, FAITHFUL AND JUST TO ME. DID THIS IN CAESAR SEEM AMBITIOUS?
WHEN THE POOR HAVE CRIED, CAESAR HATH WEPT. AMBITION SHOULD BE MADE OF STERNER STUFF!
YET BRUTUS SAYS HE WAS AMBITIOUS… AND BRUTUS IS AN HONORABLE MAN.
I SPEAK NOT TO DISPROVE WHAT BRUTUS SPOKE. I SPEAK WHAT I KNOW.

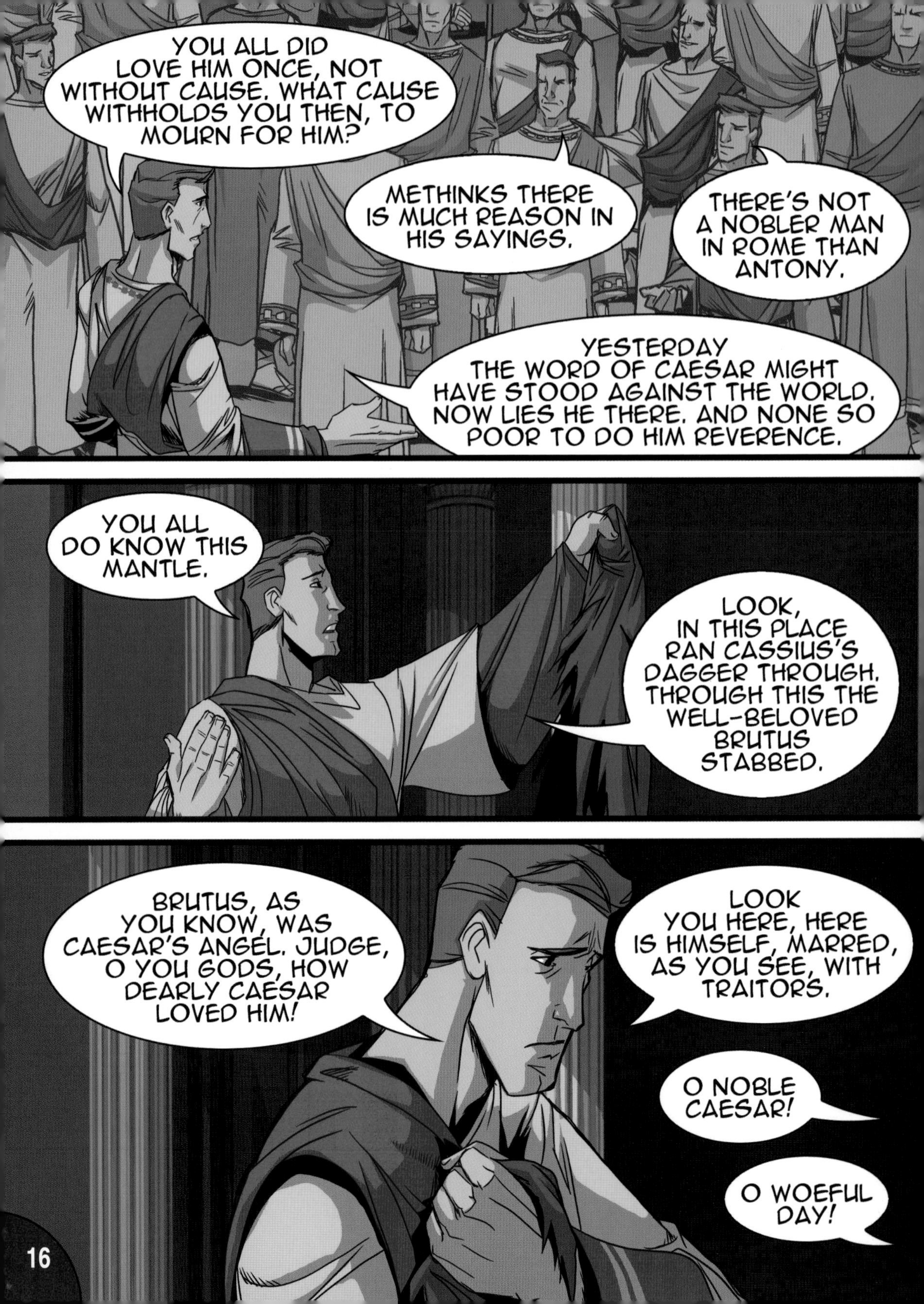
YOU ALL DID LOVE HIM ONCE, NOT WITHOUT CAUSE. WHAT CAUSE WITHHOLDS YOU THEN, TO MOURN FOR HIM?
METHINKS THERE IS MUCH REASON IN HIS SAYINGS.
THERE'S NOT A NOBLER MAN IN ROME THAN ANTONY.
YESTERDAY THE WORD OF CAESAR MIGHT HAVE STOOD AGAINST THE WORLD. NOW LIES HE THERE. AND NONE SO POOR TO DO HIM REVERENCE.
YOU ALL DO KNOW THIS MANTLE.
LOOK, IN THIS PLACE RAN CASSIUS'S DAGGER THROUGH. THROUGH THIS THE WELL-BELOVED BRUTUS STABBED.
BRUTUS, AS YOU KNOW, WAS CAESAR'S ANGEL. JUDGE, O YOU GODS, HOW DEARLY CAESAR LOVED HIM!
LOOK YOU HERE, HERE IS HIMSELF, MARRED, AS YOU SEE, WITH TRAITORS.
O NOBLE CAESAR!
O WOEFUL DAY!

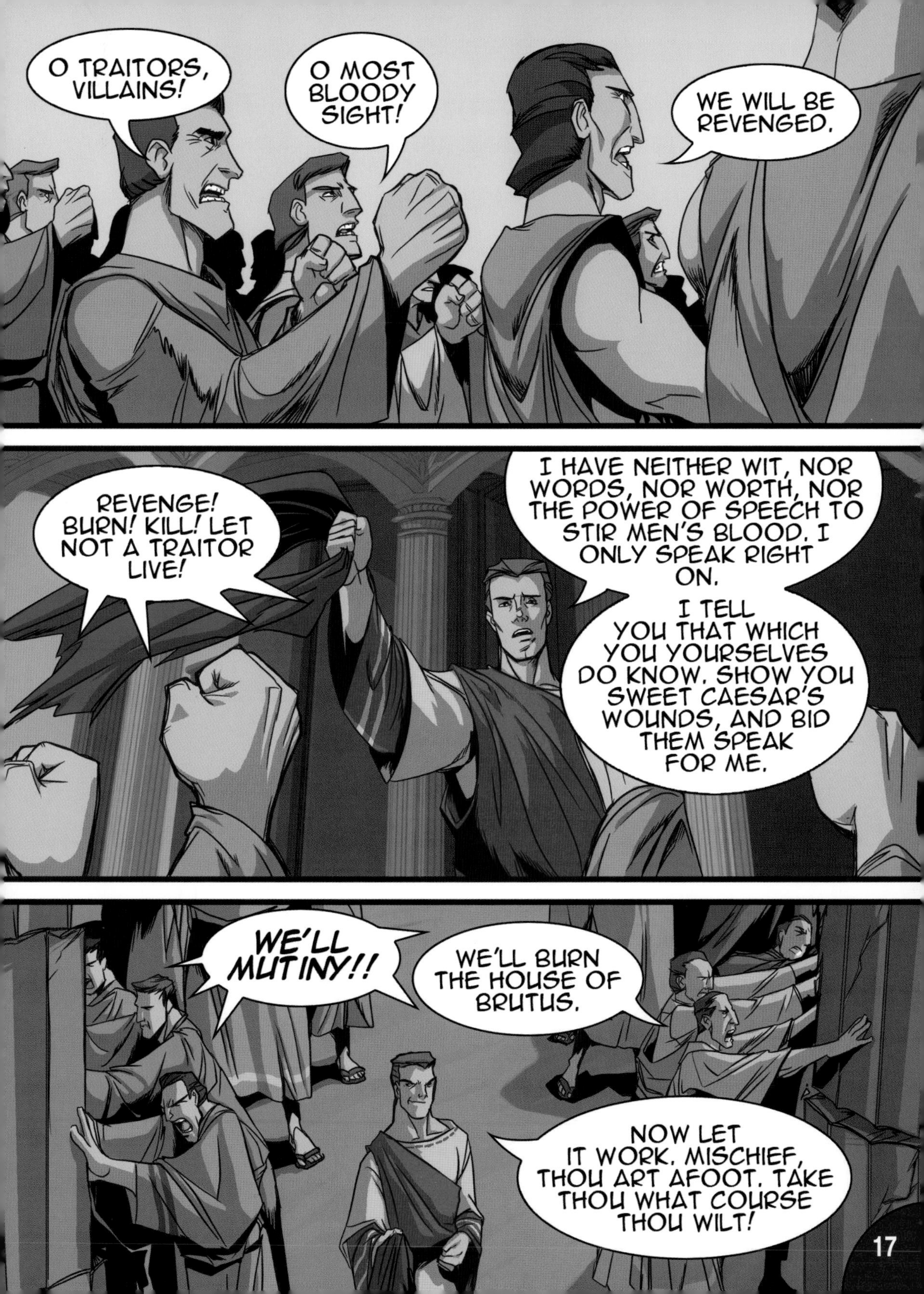
O TRAITORS, VILLAINS!
O MOST BLOODY SIGHT!
WE WILL BE REVENGED.
REVENGE! BURN! KILL! LET NOT A TRAITOR LIVE!
I HAVE NEITHER WIT, NOR WORDS, NOR WORTH, NOR THE POWER OF SPEECH TO STIR MEN'S BLOOD. I ONLY SPEAK RIGHT ON.
I TELL YOU THAT WHICH YOU YOURSELVES DO KNOW. SHOW YOU SWEET CAESAR'S WOUNDS, AND BID THEM SPEAK FOR ME.
WE'LL MUTINY!!
WE'LL BURN THE HOUSE OF BRUTUS.
NOW LET IT WORK. MISCHIEF, THOU ART AFOOT. TAKE THOU WHAT COURSE THOU WILT!

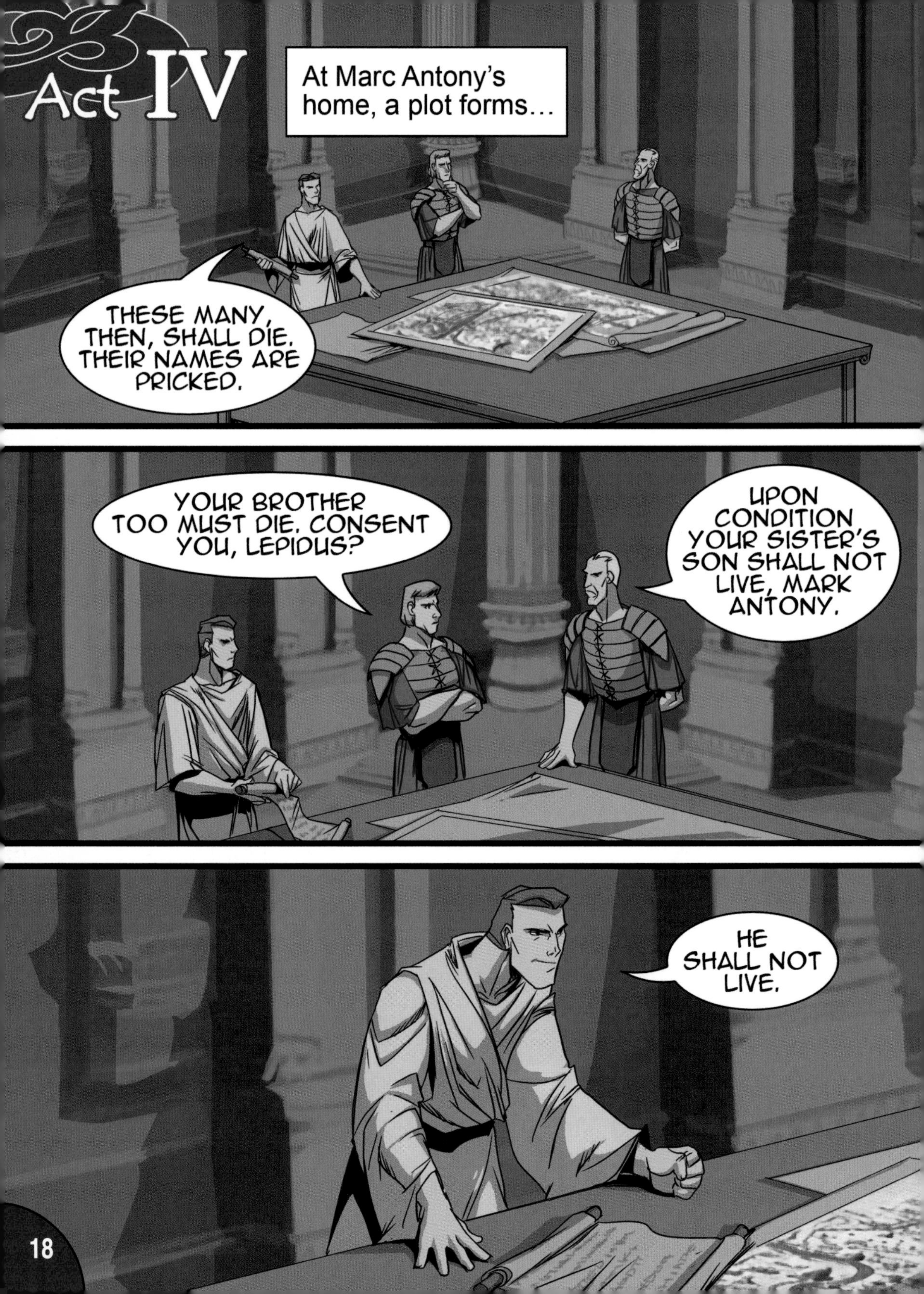
Act IV
At Marc Antony's home, a plot forms…
THESE MANY, THEN, SHALL DIE. THEIR NAMES ARE PRICKED.
YOUR BROTHER TOO MUST DIE. CONSENT YOU, LEPIDUS?
UPON CONDITION YOUR SISTER'S SON SHALL NOT LIVE, MARK ANTONY.
HE SHALL NOT LIVE.

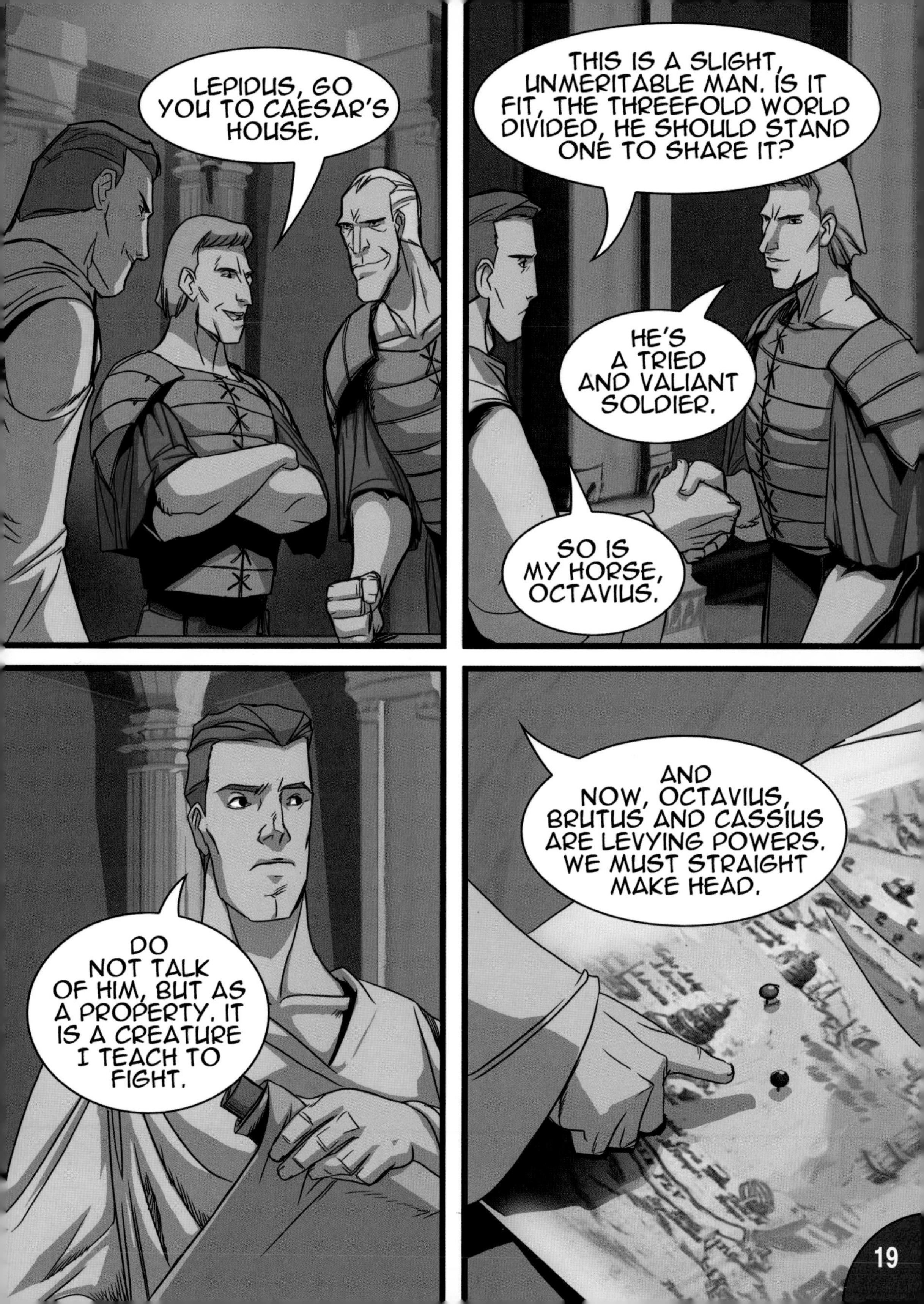
LEPIDUS, GO YOU TO CAESAR'S HOUSE.
THIS IS A SLIGHT, UNMERITABLE MAN. IS IT FIT, THE THREEFOLD WORLD DIVIDED, HE SHOULD STAND ONE TO SHARE IT?
HE'S A TRIED AND VALIANT SOLDIER.
SO IS MY HORSE, OCTAVIUS.
DO NOT TALK OF HIM, BUT AS A PROPERTY. IT IS A CREATURE I TEACH TO FIGHT.
AND NOW, OCTAVIUS, BRUTUS AND CASSIUS ARE LEVYING POWERS. WE MUST STRAIGHT MAKE HEAD.

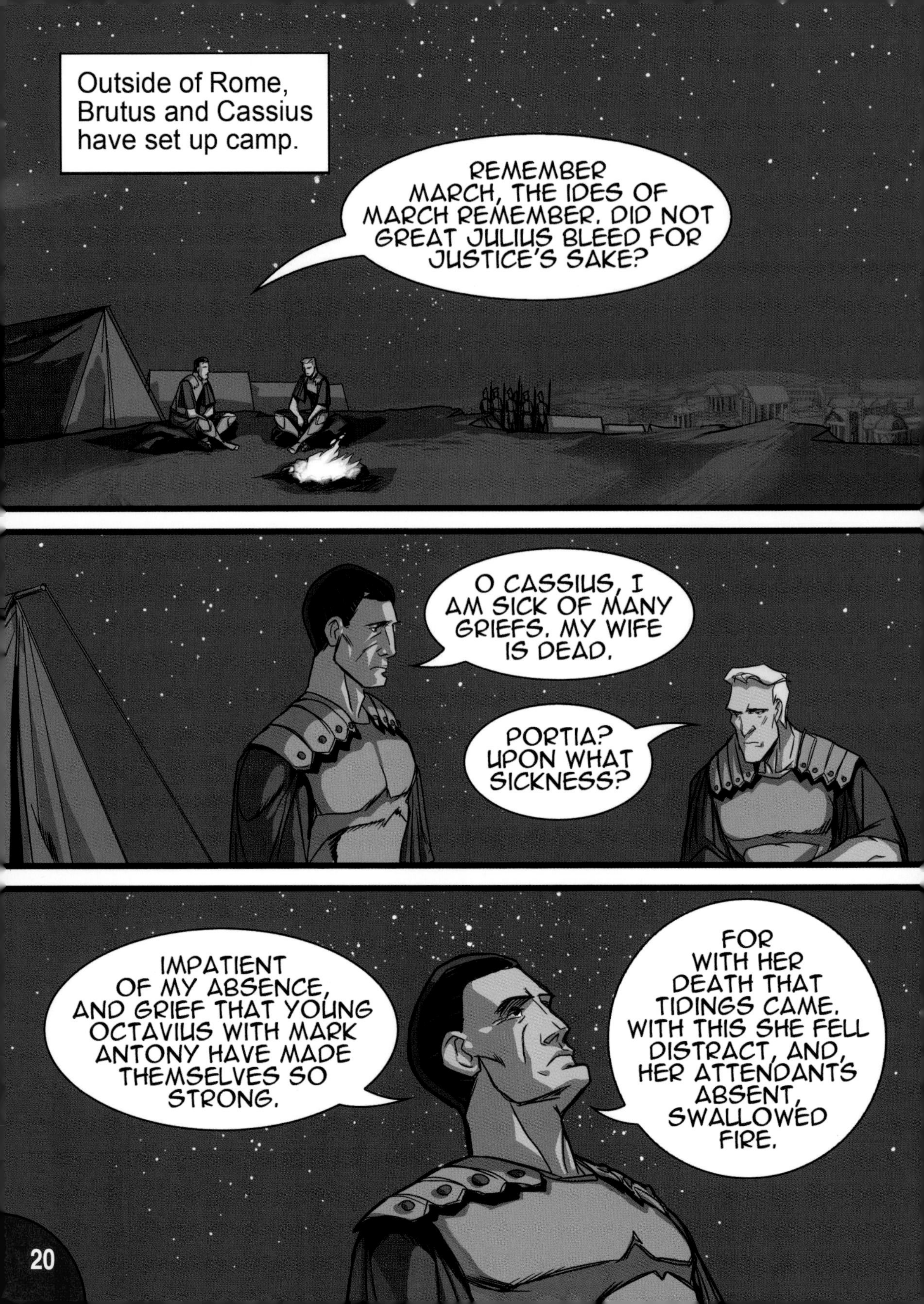
Outside of Rome, Brutus and Cassius have set up camp.
REMEMBER MARCH, THE IDES OF MARCH REMEMBER. DID NOT GREAT JULIUS BLEED FOR JUSTICE'S SAKE?
O CASSIUS, I AM SICK OF MANY GRIEFS. MY WIFE IS DEAD.
PORTIA? UPON WHAT SICKNESS?
IMPATIENT OF MY ABSENCE, AND GRIEF THAT YOUNG OCTAVIUS WITH MARK ANTONY HAVE MADE THEMSELVES SO STRONG.
FOR WITH HER DEATH THAT TIDINGS CAME. WITH THIS SHE FELL DISTRACT, AND, HER ATTENDANTS ABSENT, SWALLOWED FIRE.

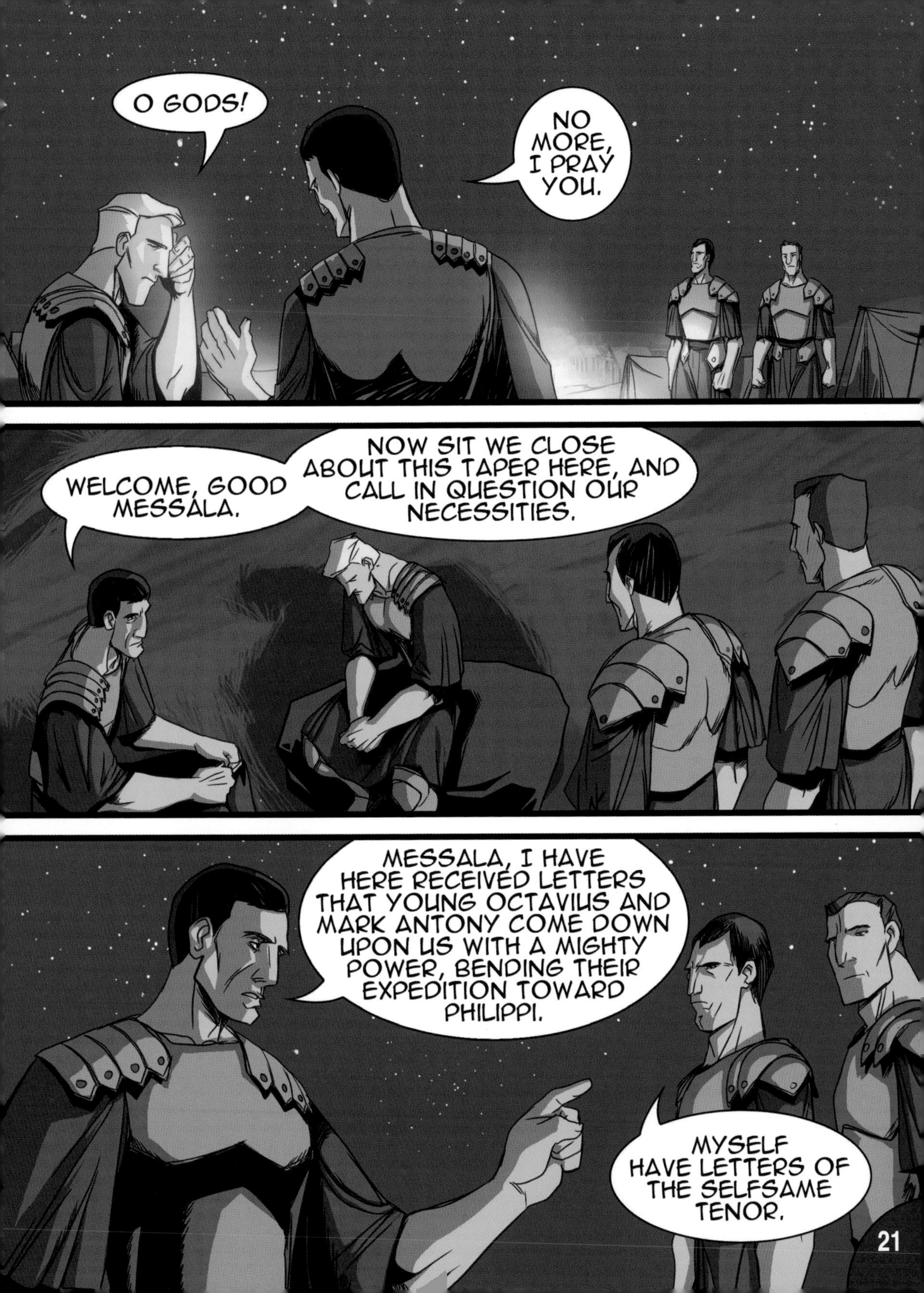
O GODS!
NO MORE, I PRAY YOU.
WELCOME, GOOD MESSALA.
NOW SIT WE CLOSE ABOUT THIS TAPER HERE, AND CALL IN QUESTION OUR NECESSITIES.
MESSALA, I HAVE HERE RECEIVED LETTERS THAT YOUNG OCTAVIUS AND MARK ANTONY COME DOWN UPON US WITH A MIGHTY POWER, BENDING THEIR EXPEDITION TOWARD PHILIPPI.
MYSELF HAVE LETTERS OF THE SELFSAME TENOR.

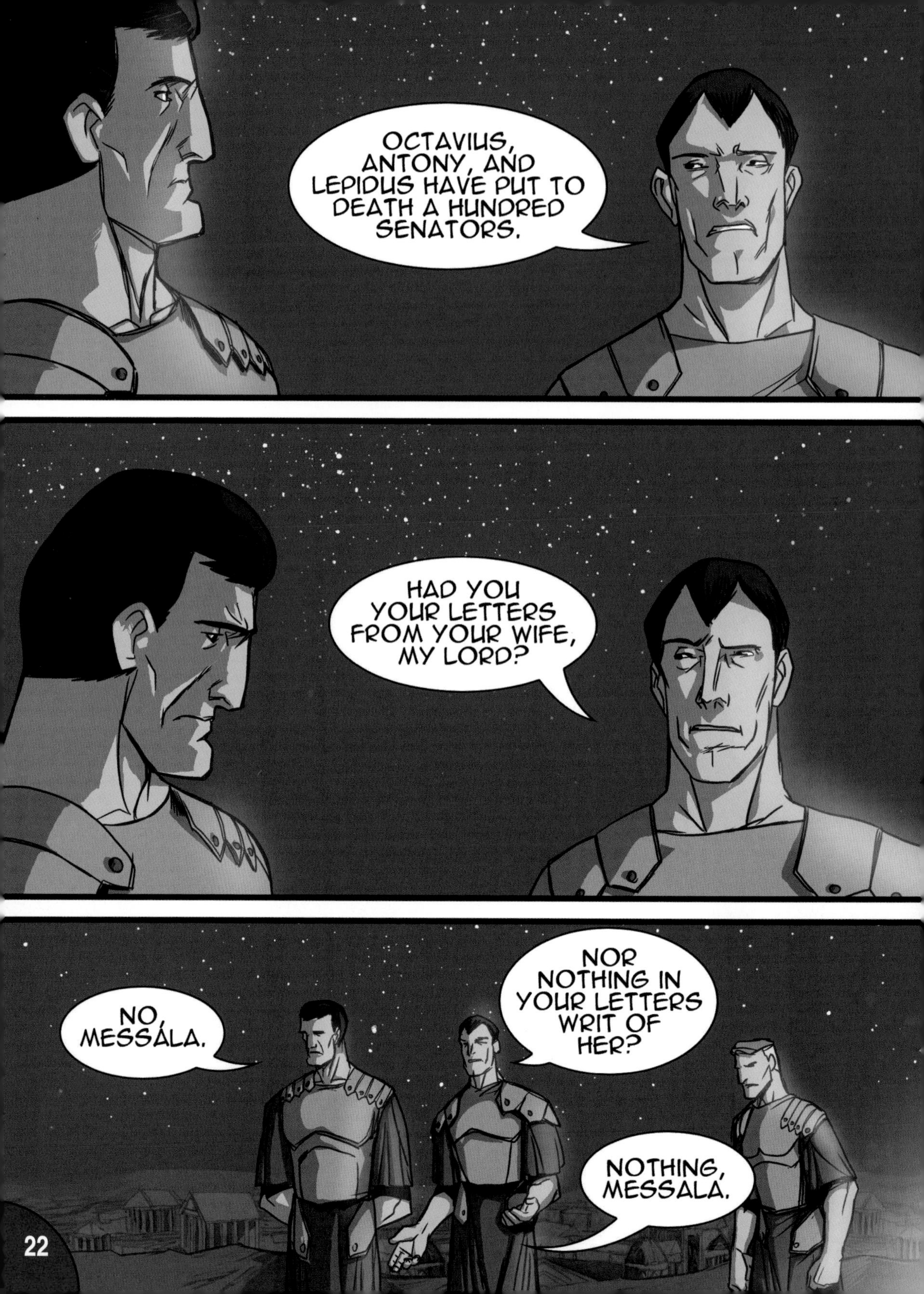
OCTAVIUS, ANTONY, AND LEPIDUS HAVE PUT TO DEATH A HUNDRED SENATORS.
HAD YOU YOUR LETTERS FROM YOUR WIFE, MY LORD?
NO, MESSALA.
NOR NOTHING IN YOUR LETTERS WRIT OF HER?
NOTHING, MESSALA.

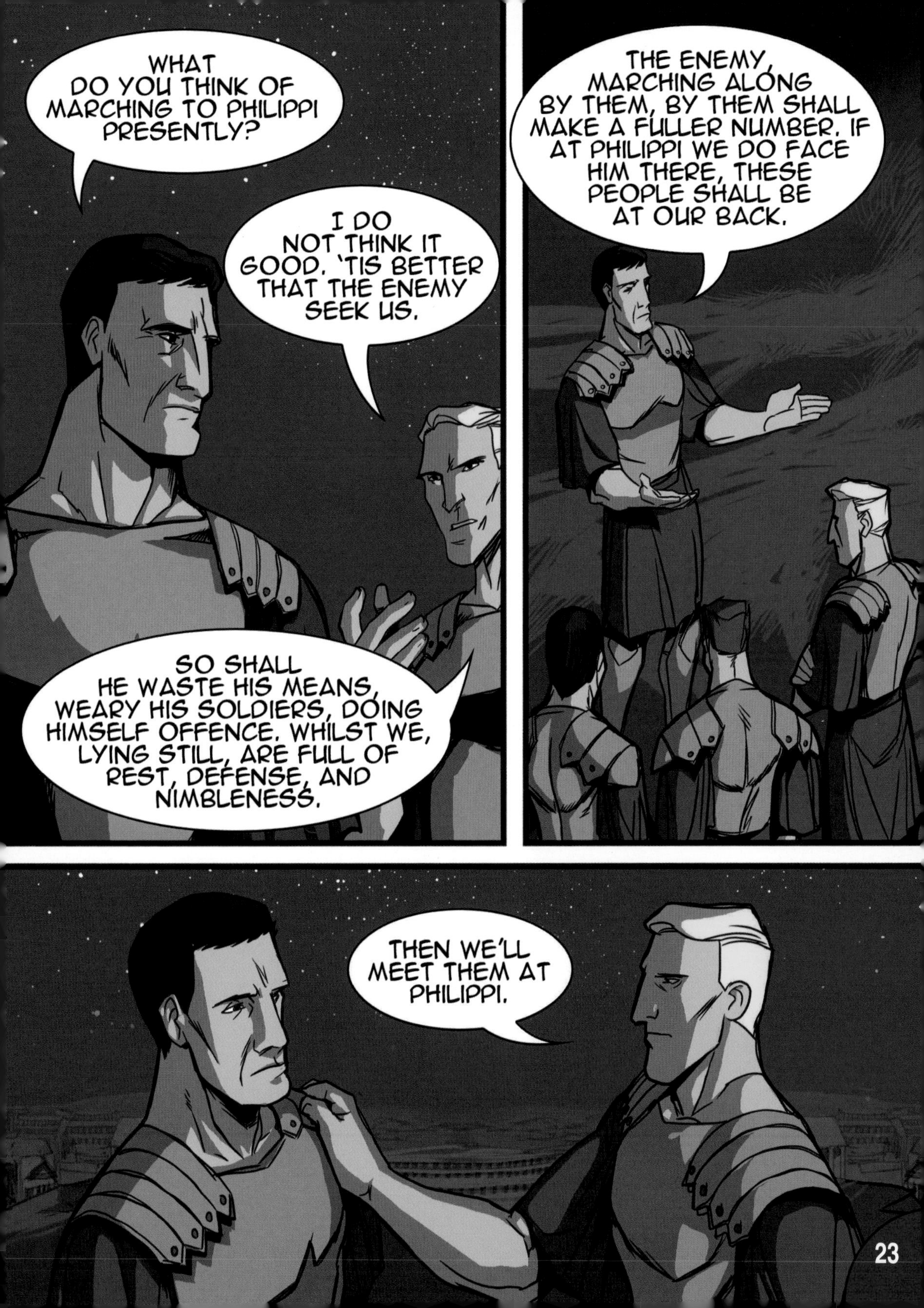
WHAT DO YOU THINK OF MARCHING TO PHILIPPI PRESENTLY?
I DO NOT THINK IT GOOD. 'TIS BETTER THAT THE ENEMY SEEK US.
SO SHALL HE WASTE HIS MEANS, WEARY HIS SOLDIERS, DOING HIMSELF OFFENCE. WHILST WE, LYING STILL, ARE FULL OF REST, DEFENSE, AND NIMBLENESS.
THE ENEMY, MARCHING ALONG BY THEM, BY THEM SHALL MAKE A FULLER NUMBER. IF AT PHILIPPI WE DO FACE HIM THERE, THESE PEOPLE SHALL BE AT OUR BACK.
THEN WE'LL MEET THEM AT PHILIPPI.

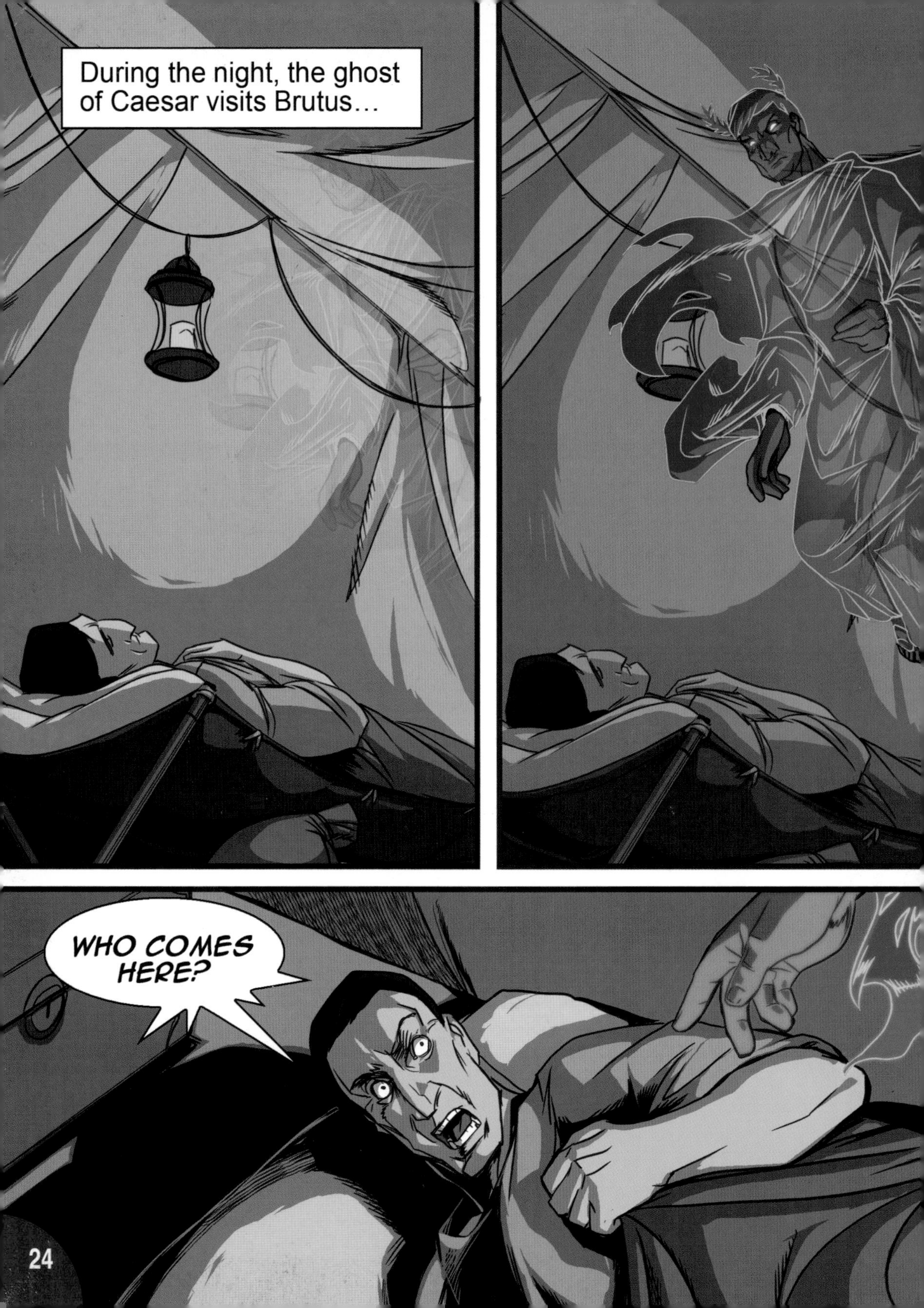
During the night, the ghost of Caesar visits Brutus…
WHO COMES HERE?

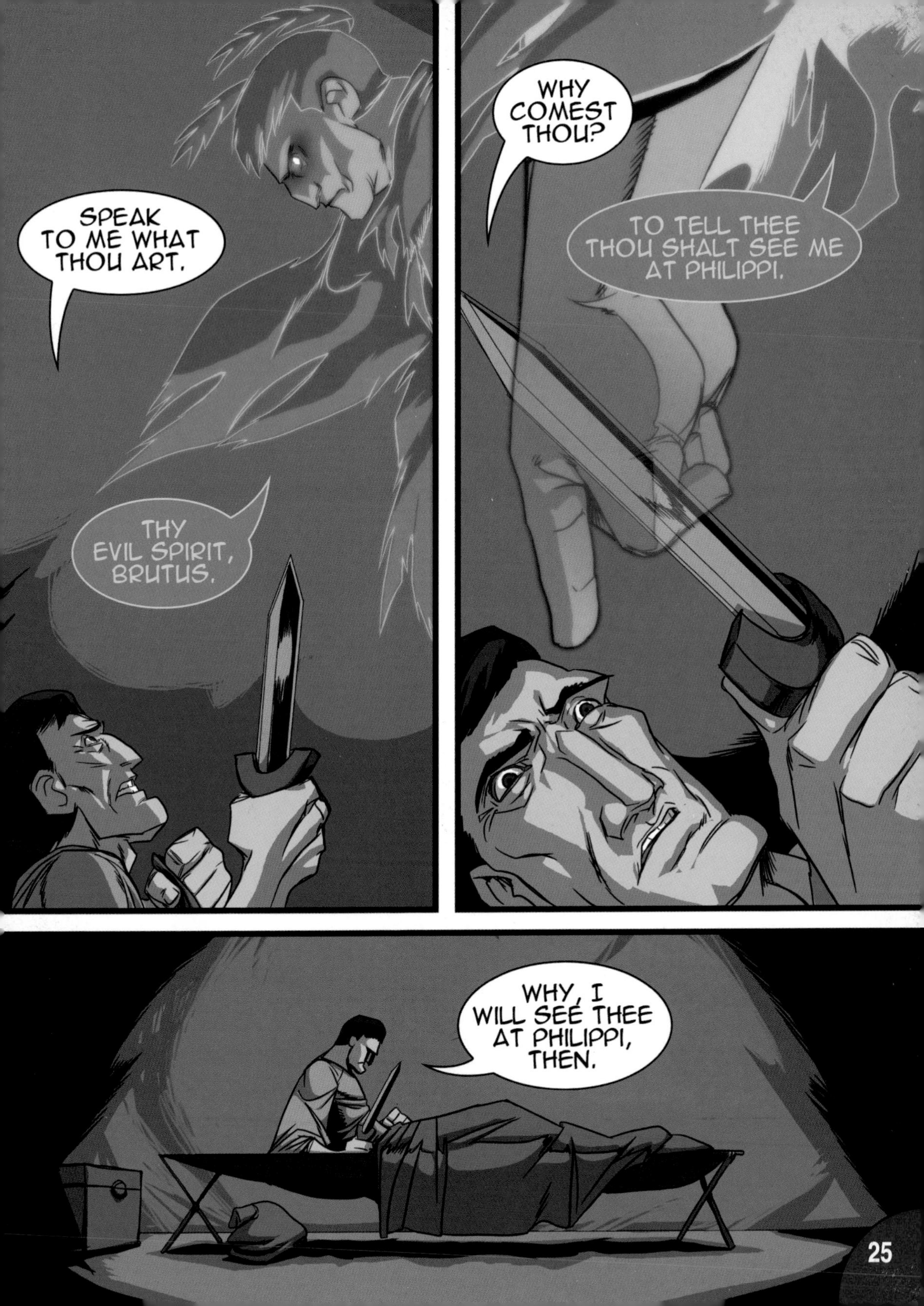
SPEAK TO ME WHAT THOU ART.
THY EVIL SPIRIT, BRUTUS.
WHY COMEST THOU?
TO TELL THEE THOU SHALT SEE ME AT PHILIPPI.
WHY, I WILL SEE THEE AT PHILIPPI, THEN.

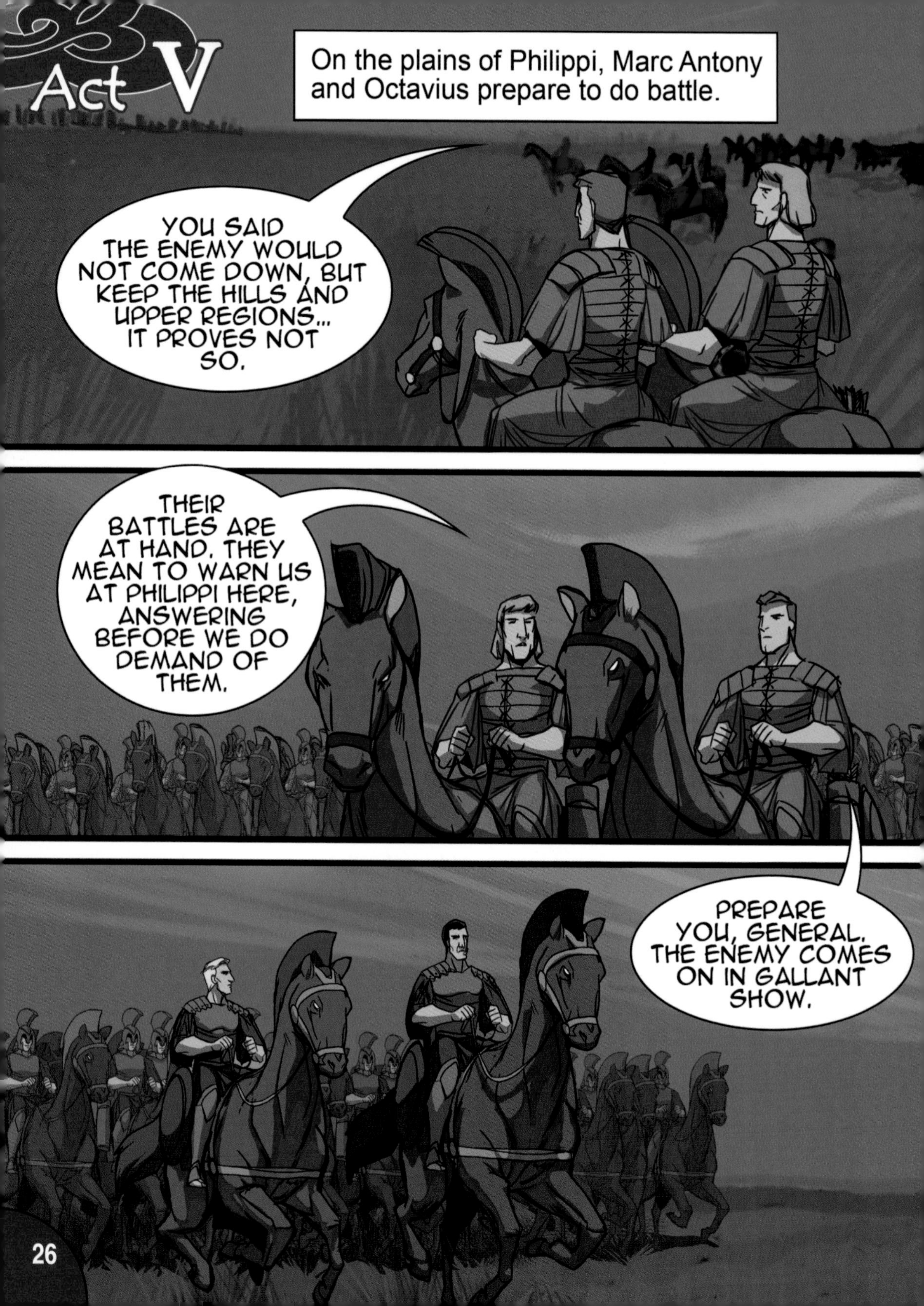
Act V
On the plains of Philippi, Marc Antony and Octavius prepare to do battle.
YOU SAID THE ENEMY WOULD NOT COME DOWN, BUT KEEP THE HILLS AND UPPER REGIONS... IT PROVES NOT SO.
THEIR BATTLES ARE AT HAND. THEY MEAN TO WARN US AT PHILIPPI HERE, ANSWERING BEFORE WE DO DEMAND OF THEM.
PREPARE YOU, GENERAL. THE ENEMY COMES ON IN GALLANT SHOW.

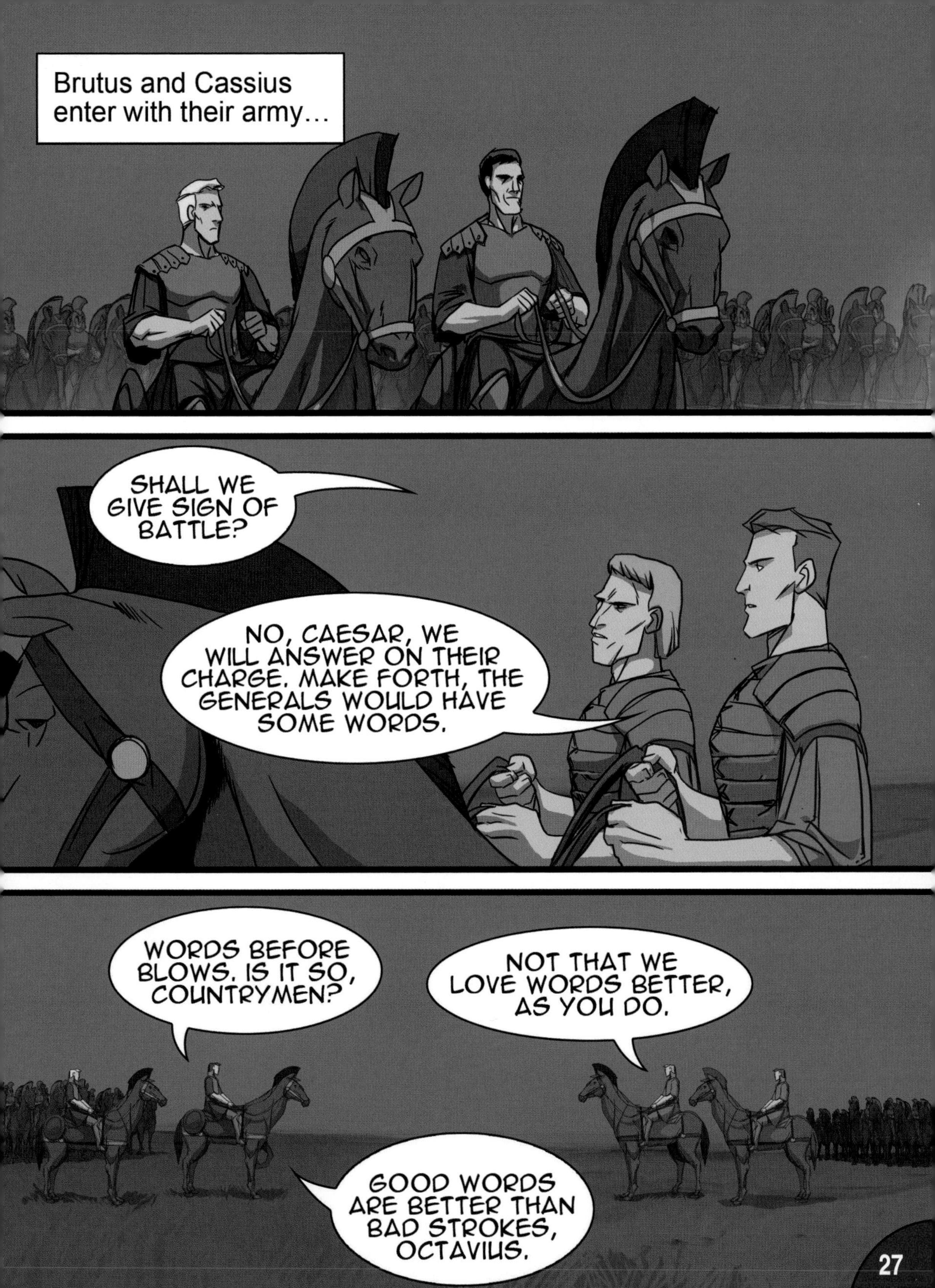
Brutus and Cassius enter with their army…
SHALL WE GIVE SIGN OF BATTLE?
NO, CAESAR, WE WILL ANSWER ON THEIR CHARGE. MAKE FORTH, THE GENERALS WOULD HAVE SOME WORDS.
WORDS BEFORE BLOWS. IS IT SO, COUNTRYMEN?
NOT THAT WE LOVE WORDS BETTER, AS YOU DO.
GOOD WORDS ARE BETTER THAN BAD STROKES, OCTAVIUS.

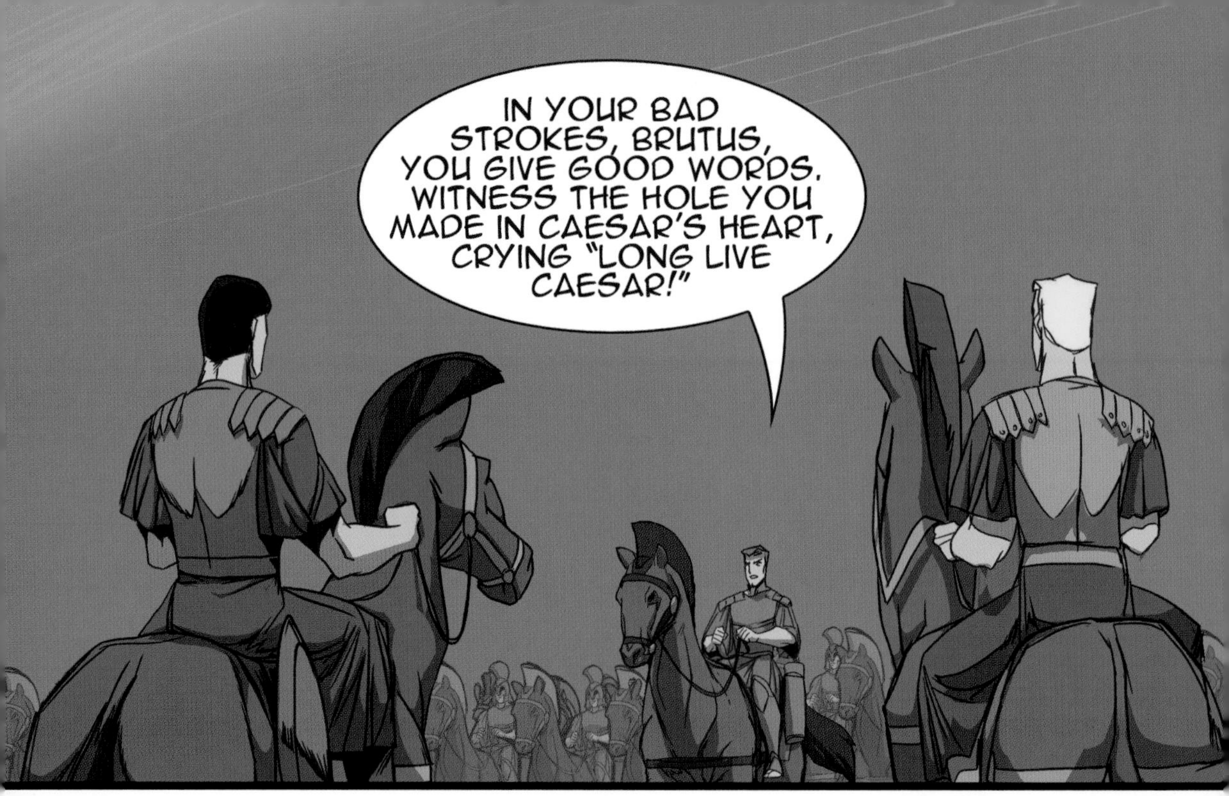
IN YOUR BAD STROKES, BRUTUS, YOU GIVE GOOD WORDS. WITNESS THE HOLE YOU MADE IN CAESAR'S HEART, CRYING "LONG LIVE CAESAR!"

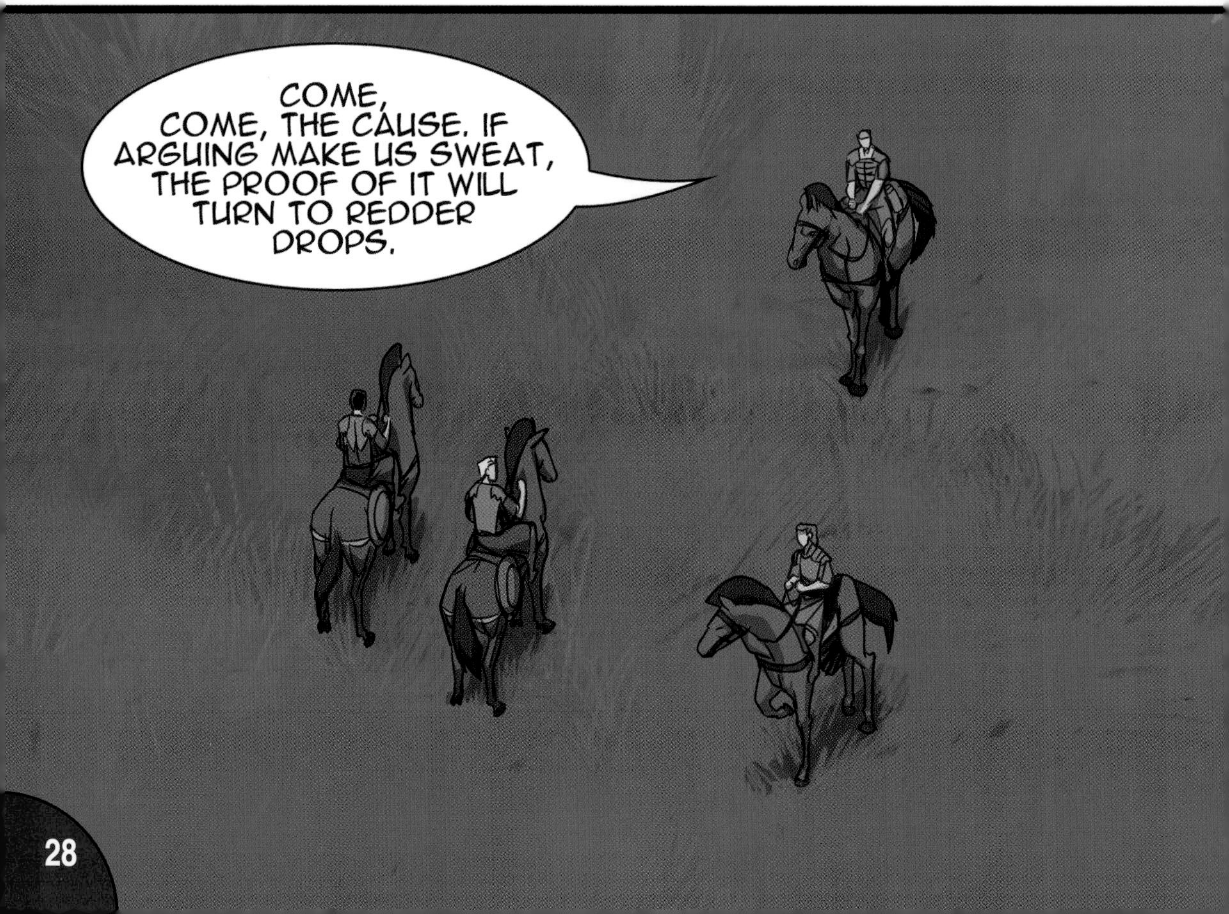
COME, COME, THE CAUSE. IF ARGUING MAKE US SWEAT, THE PROOF OF IT WILL TURN TO REDDER DROPS.

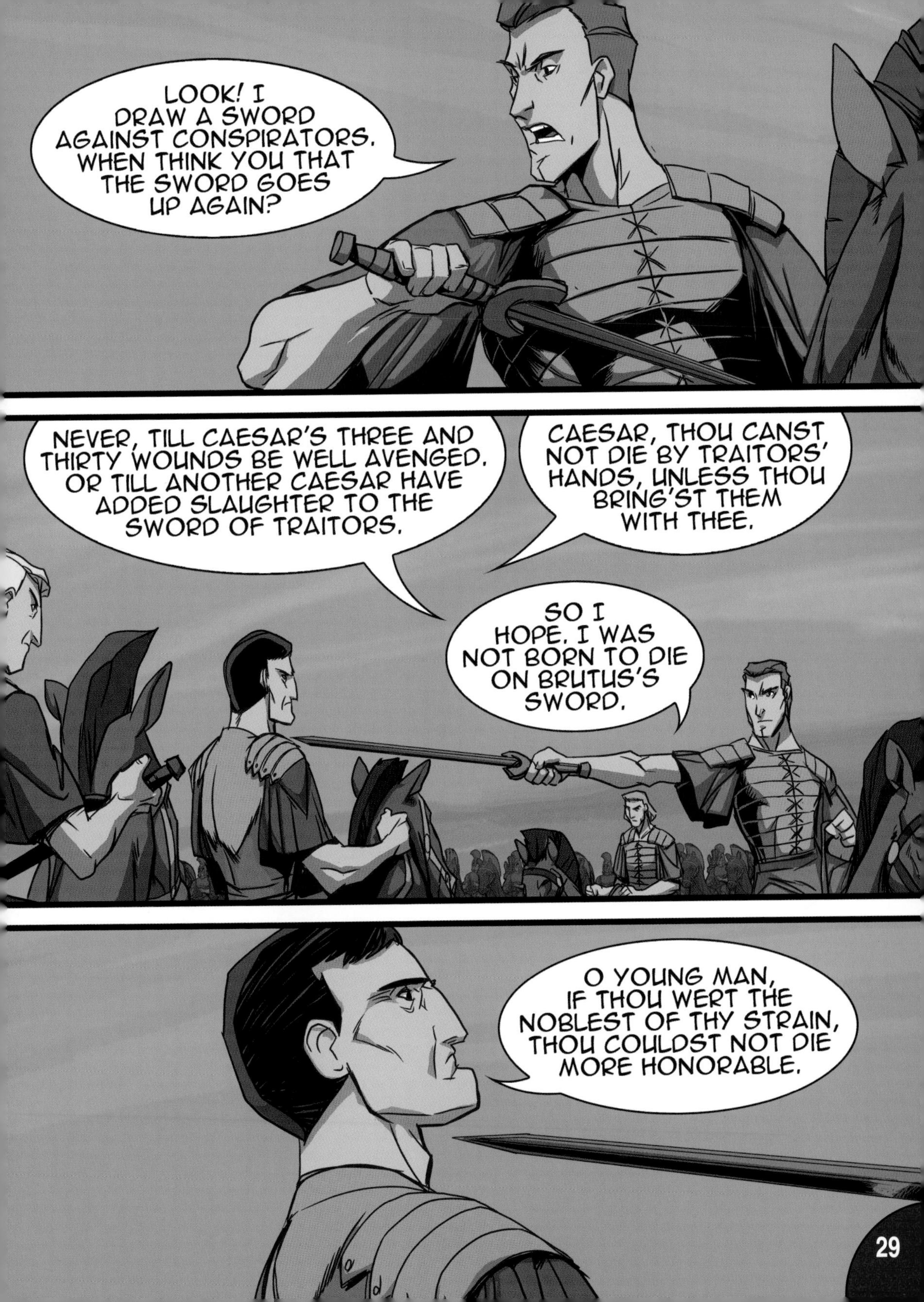
LOOK! I DRAW A SWORD AGAINST CONSPIRATORS. WHEN THINK YOU THAT THE SWORD GOES UP AGAIN?
NEVER, TILL CAESAR'S THREE AND THIRTY WOUNDS BE WELL AVENGED, OR TILL ANOTHER CAESAR HAVE ADDED SLAUGHTER TO THE SWORD OF TRAITORS.
CAESAR, THOU CANST NOT DIE BY TRAITORS' HANDS, UNLESS THOU BRING'ST THEM WITH THEE.
SO I HOPE. I WAS NOT BORN TO DIE ON BRUTUS'S SWORD.
O YOUNG MAN, IF THOU WERT THE NOBLEST OF THY STRAIN, THOU COULDST NOT DIE MORE HONORABLE.

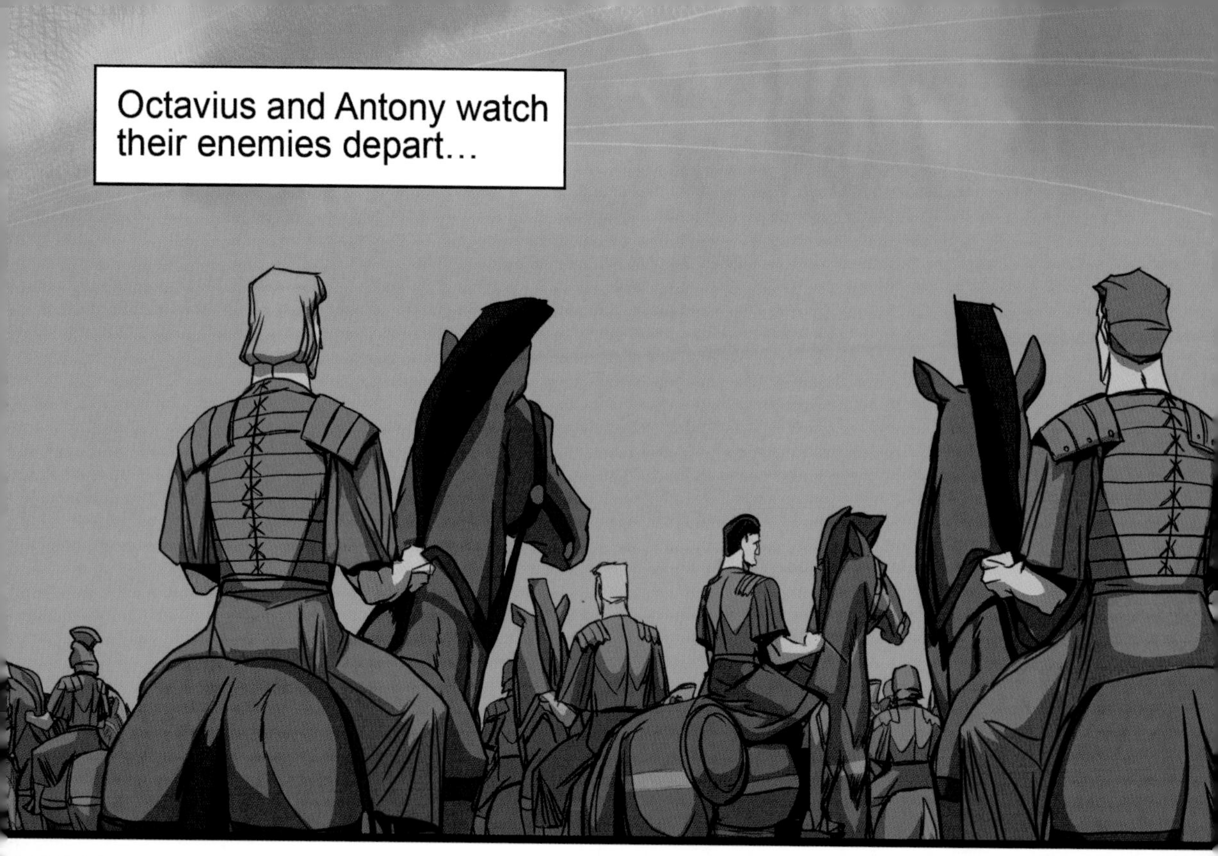
Octavius and Antony watch their enemies depart…

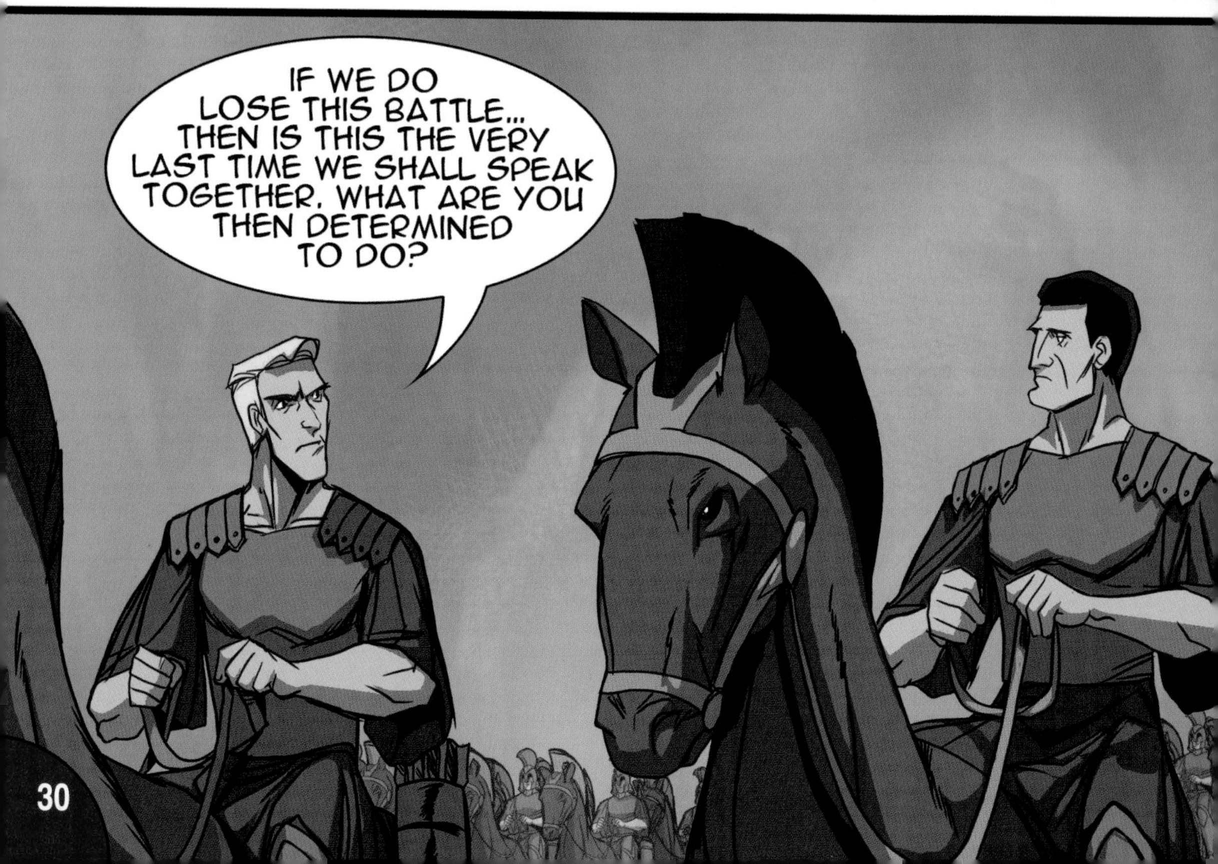
IF WE DO LOSE THIS BATTLE... THEN IS THIS THE VERY LAST TIME WE SHALL SPEAK TOGETHER. WHAT ARE YOU THEN DETERMINED TO DO?

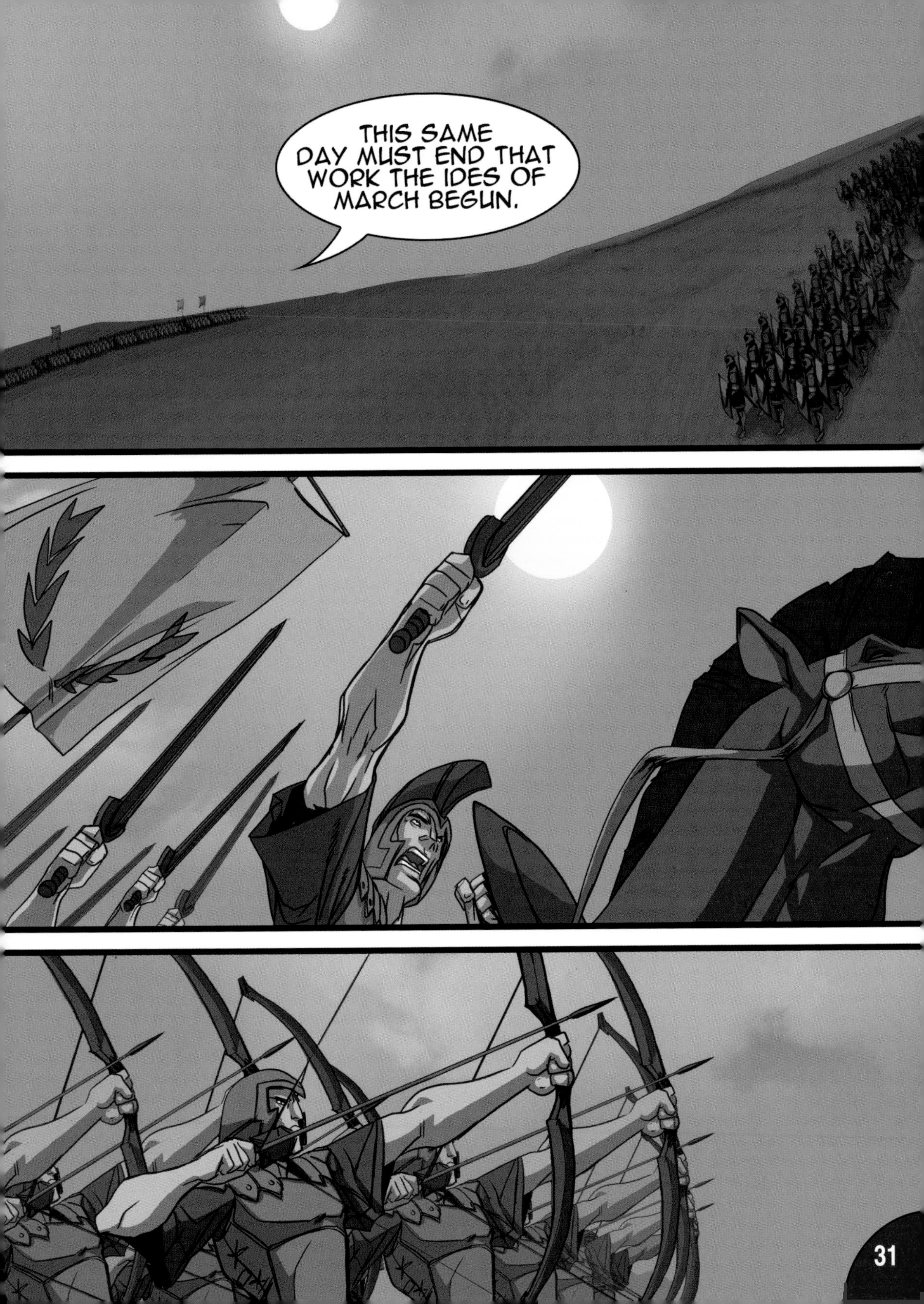
THIS SAME DAY MUST END THAT WORK THE IDES OF MARCH BEGUN.

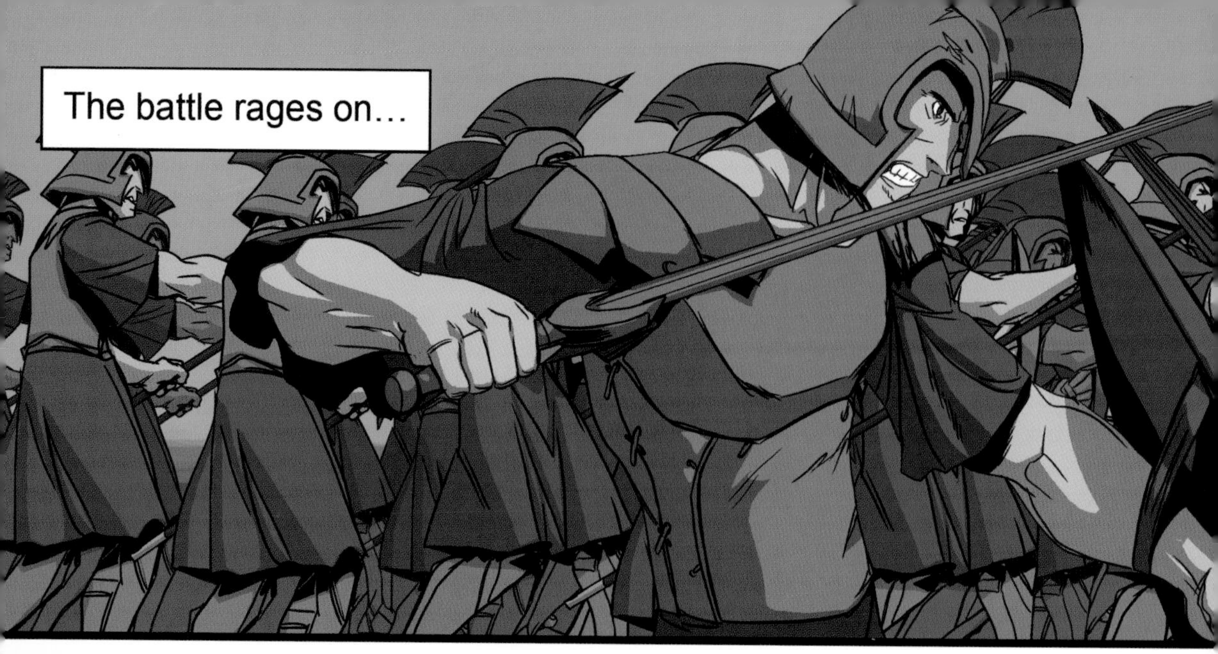
The battle rages on…

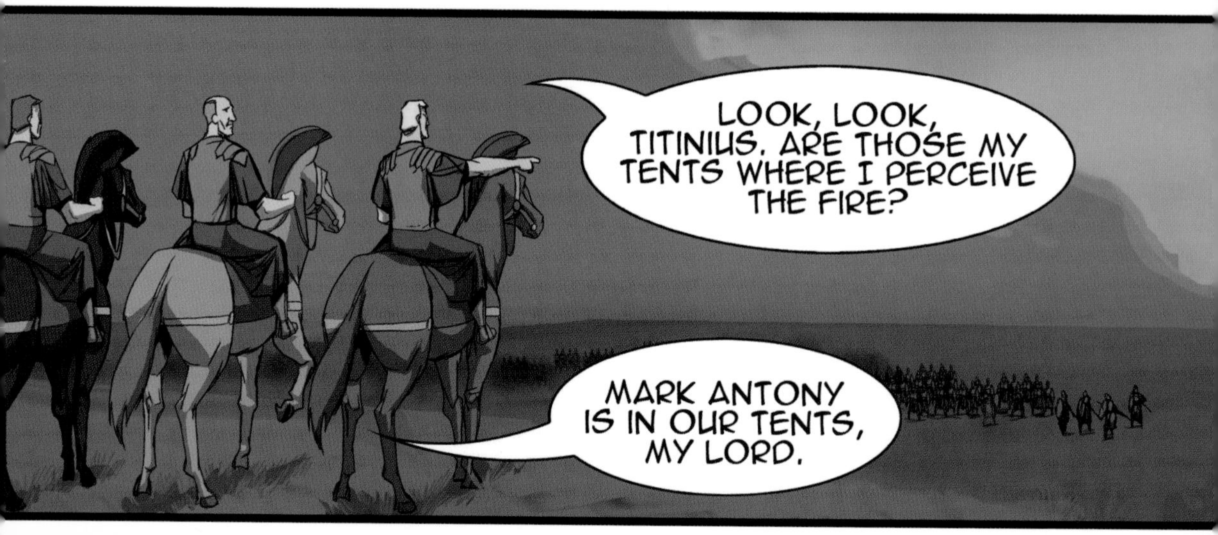
LOOK, LOOK, TITINIUS. ARE THOSE MY TENTS WHERE I PERCEIVE THE FIRE?
MARK ANTONY IS IN OUR TENTS, MY LORD.

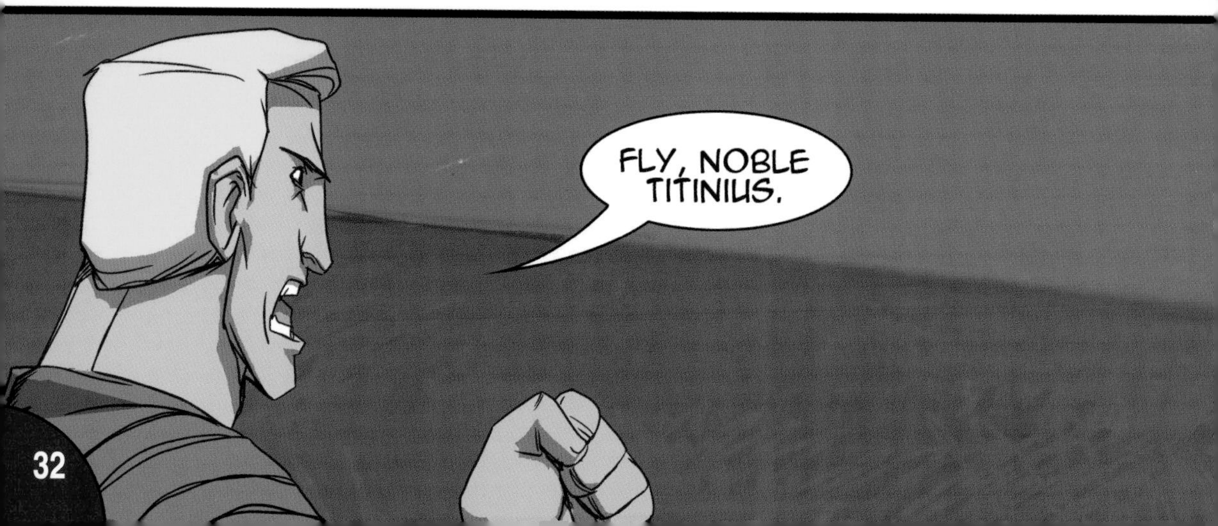
FLY, NOBLE TITINIUS.

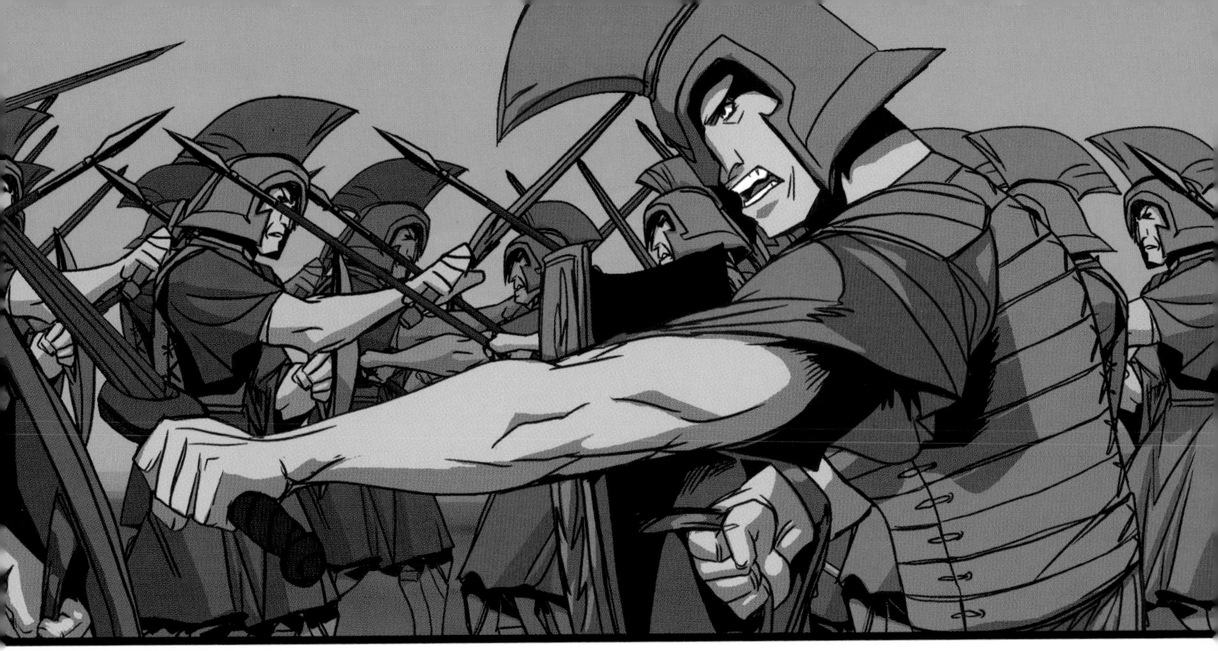
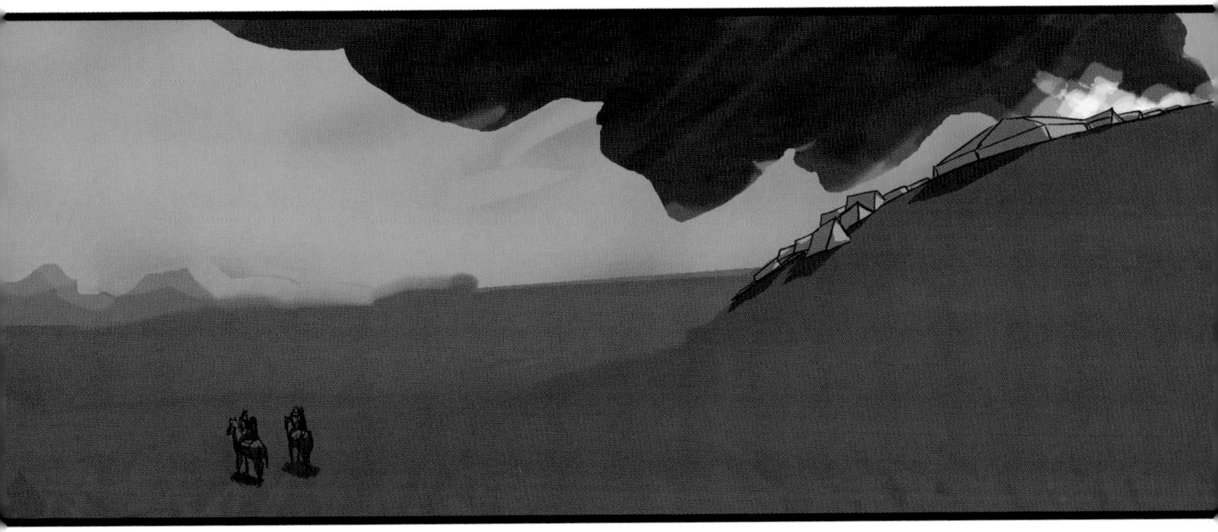
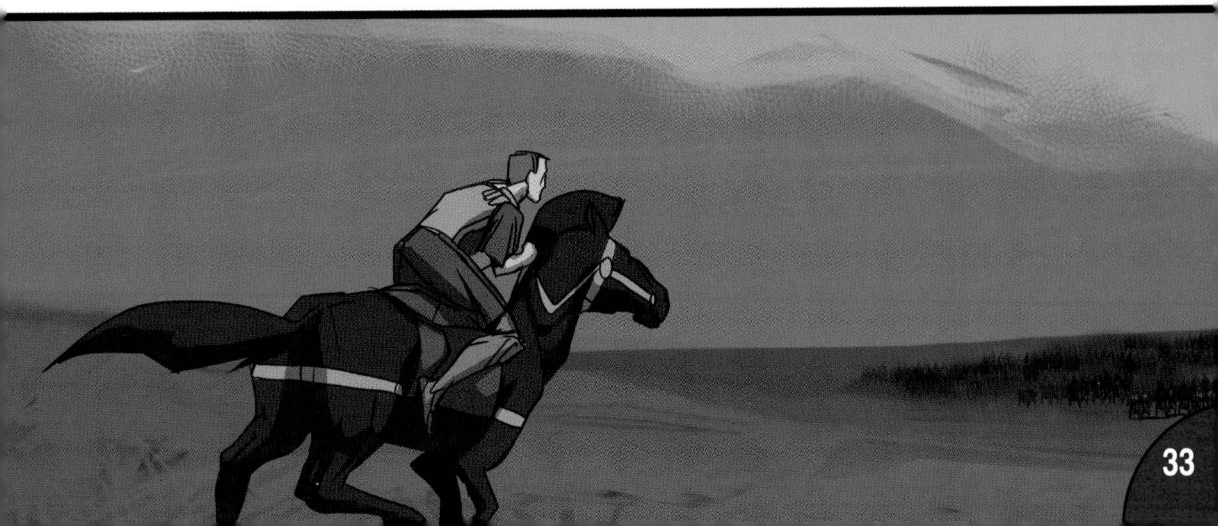

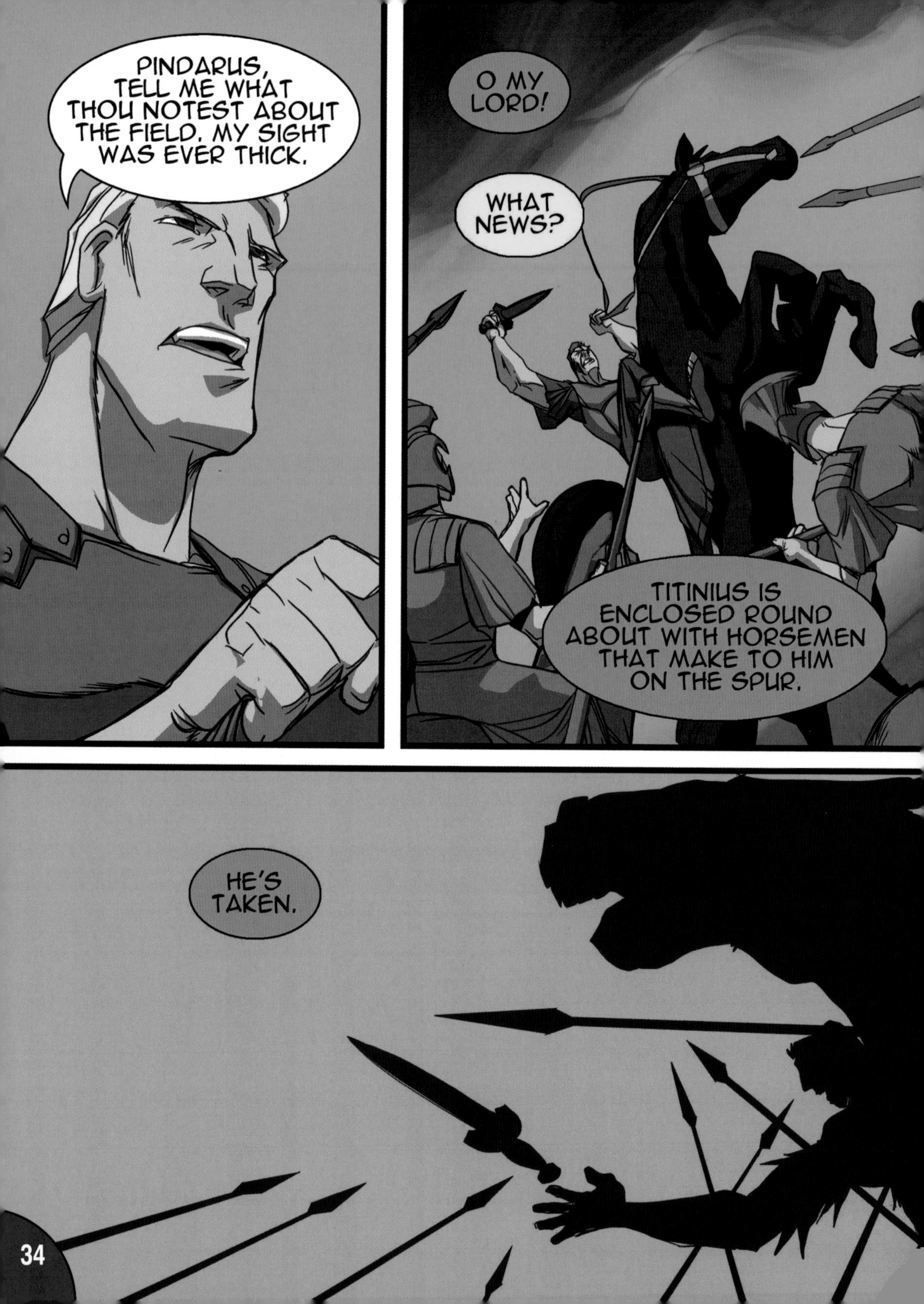
PINDARUS, TELL ME WHAT THOU NOTEST ABOUT THE FIELD. MY SIGHT WAS EVER THICK.
O MY LORD!
WHAT NEWS?
TITINIUS IS ENCLOSED ROUND ABOUT WITH HORSEMEN THAT MAKE TO HIM ON THE SPUR.
HE'S TAKEN.

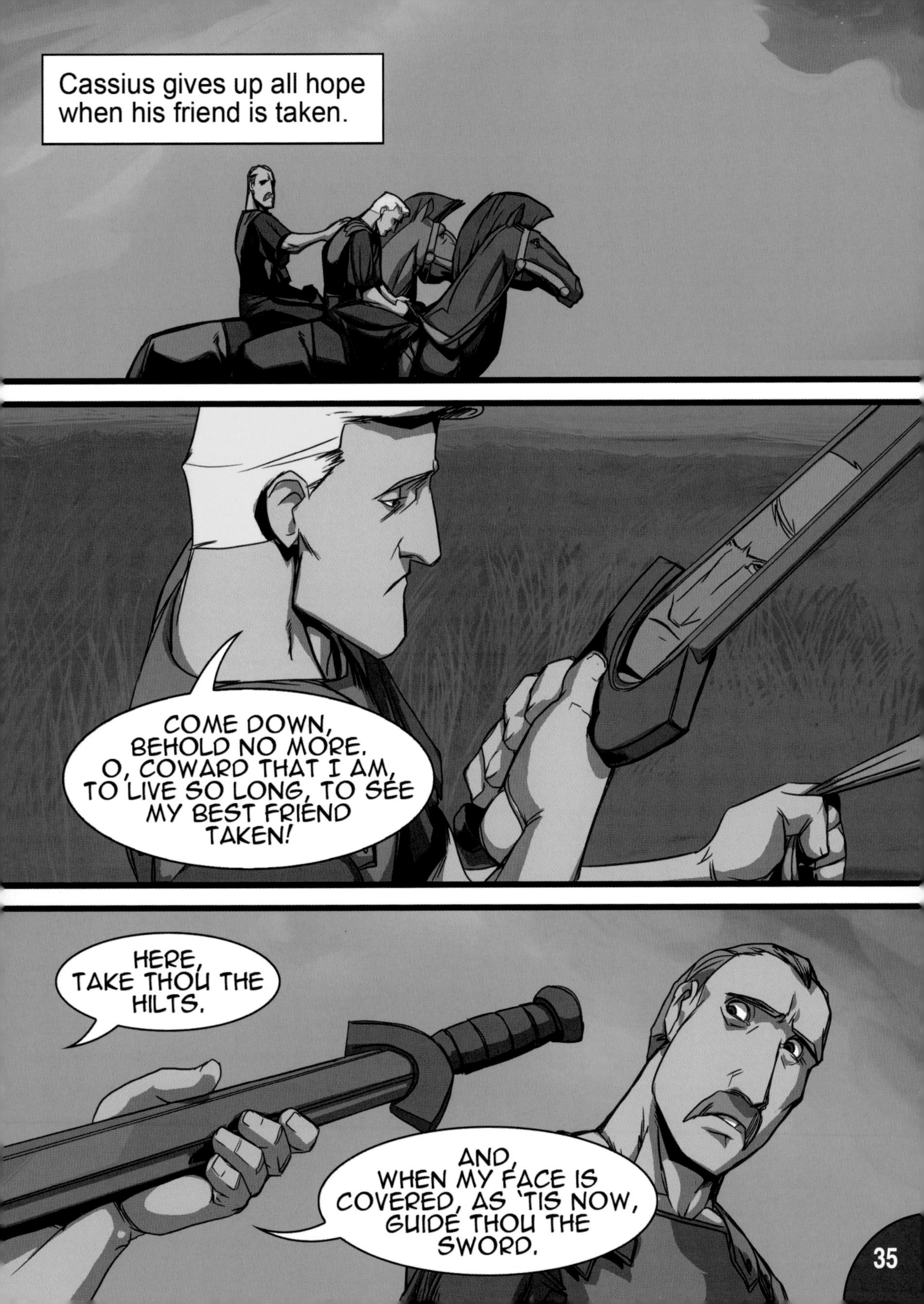
Cassius gives up all hope when his friend is taken.
COME DOWN, BEHOLD NO MORE. O, COWARD THAT I AM, TO LIVE SO LONG, TO SEE MY BEST FRIEND TAKEN!
HERE, TAKE THOU THE HILTS.
AND, WHEN MY FACE IS COVERED, AS 'TIS NOW, GUIDE THOU THE SWORD.

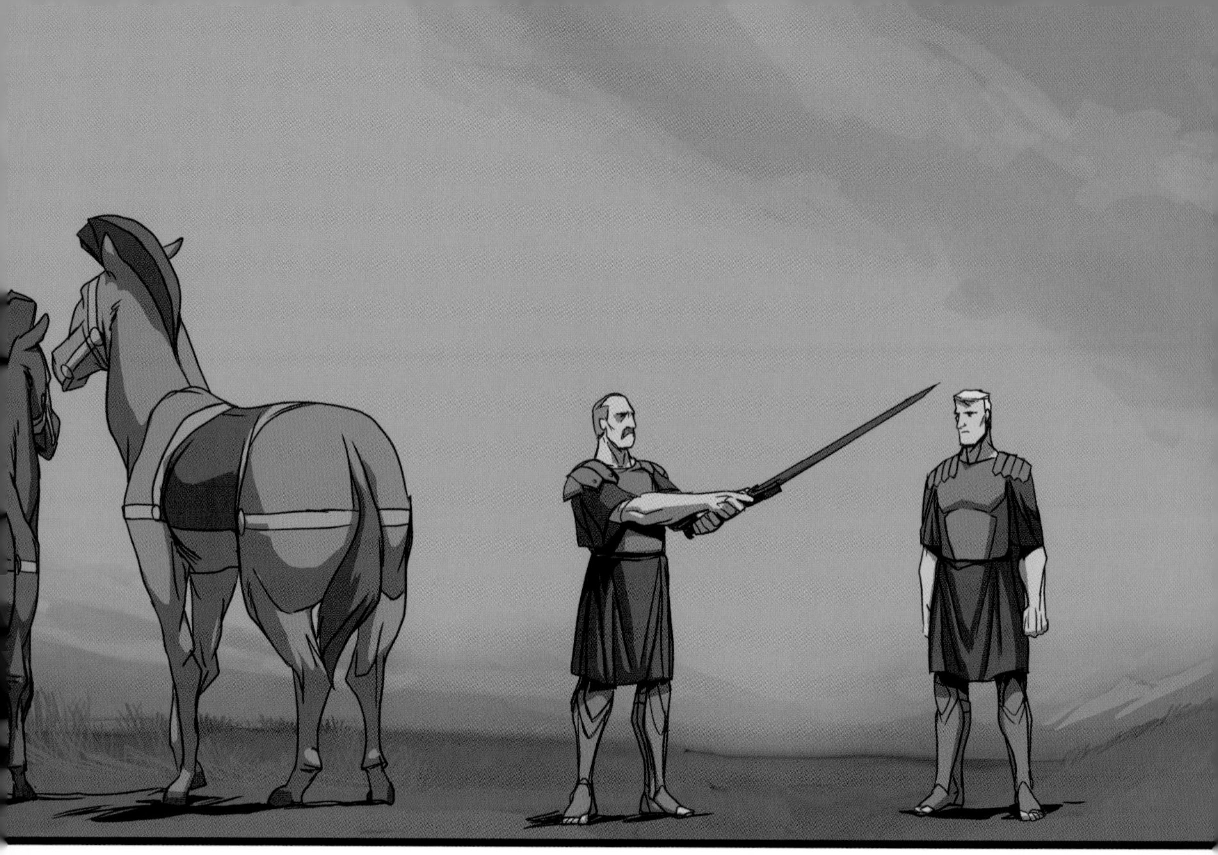

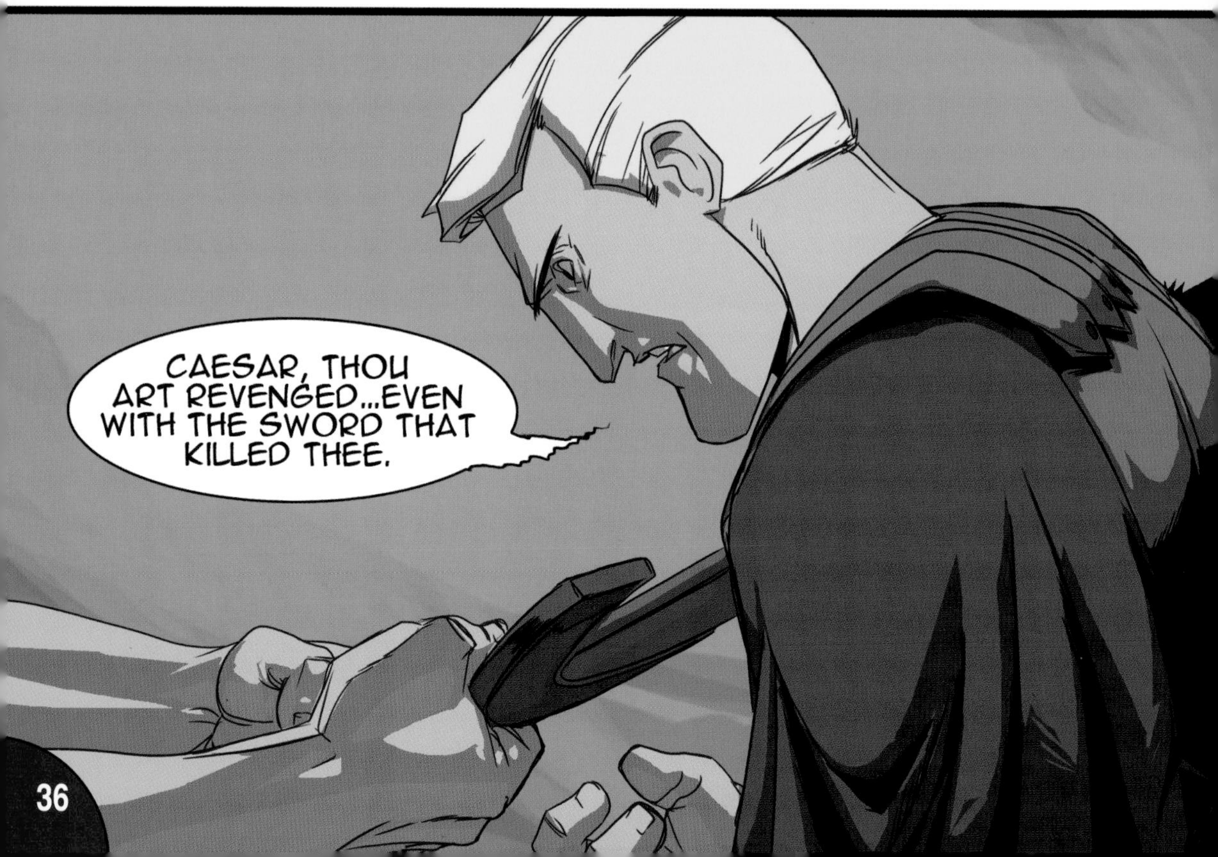
CAESAR, THOU ART REVENGED...EVEN WITH THE SWORD THAT KILLED THEE.

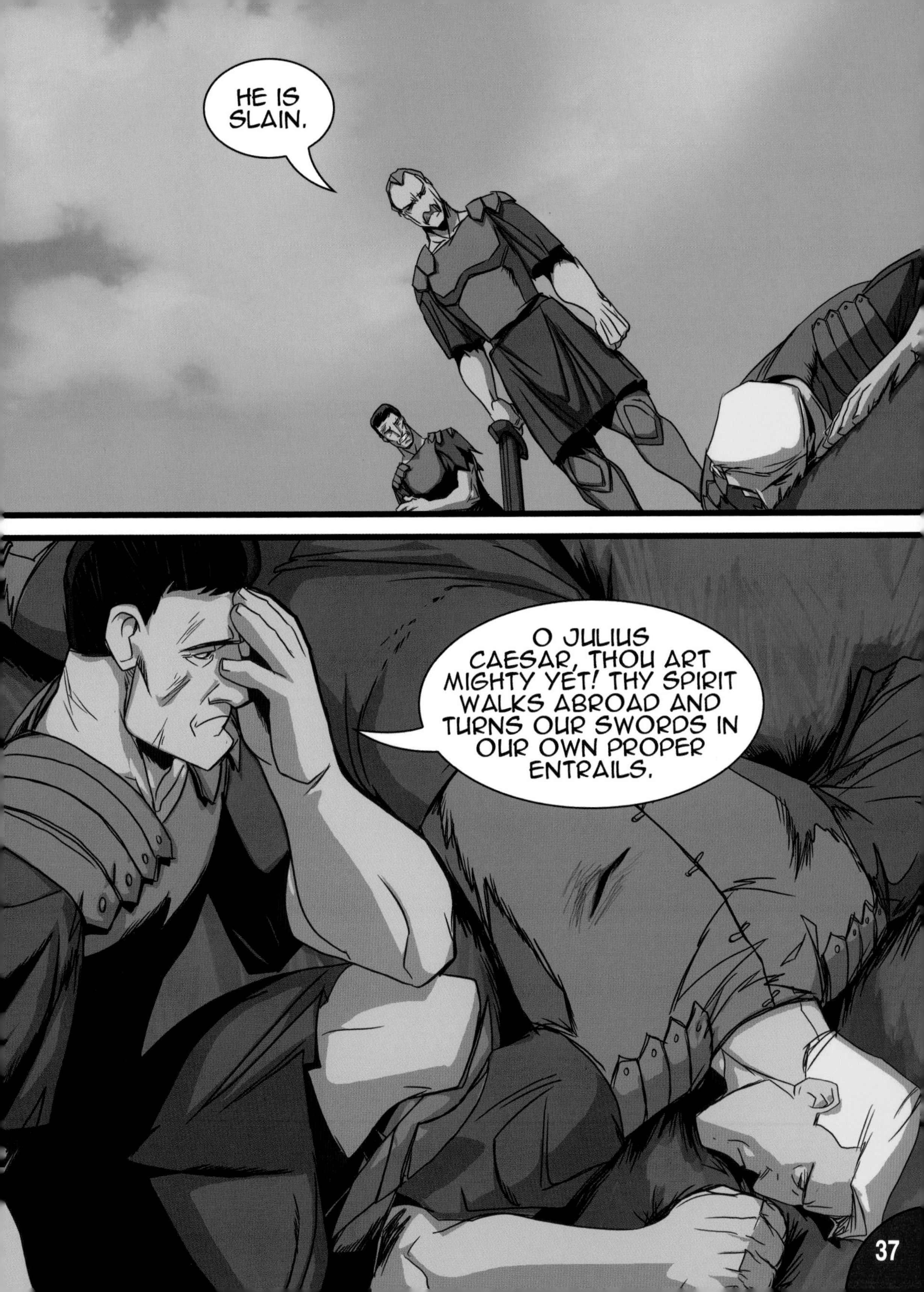
HE IS SLAIN.
O JULIUS CAESAR, THOU ART MIGHTY YET! THY SPIRIT WALKS ABROAD AND TURNS OUR SWORDS IN OUR OWN PROPER ENTRAILS.

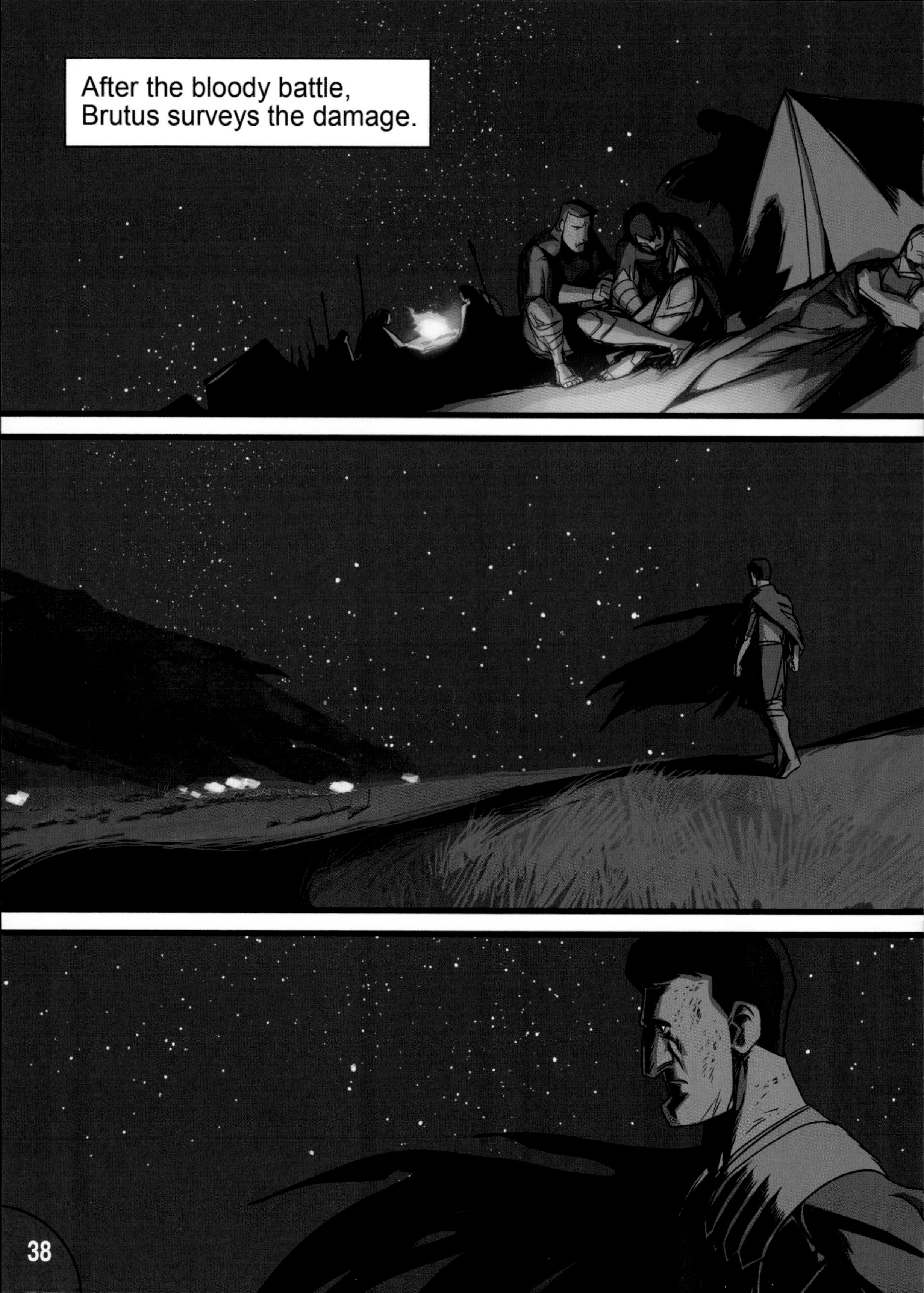
After the bloody battle, Brutus surveys the damage.

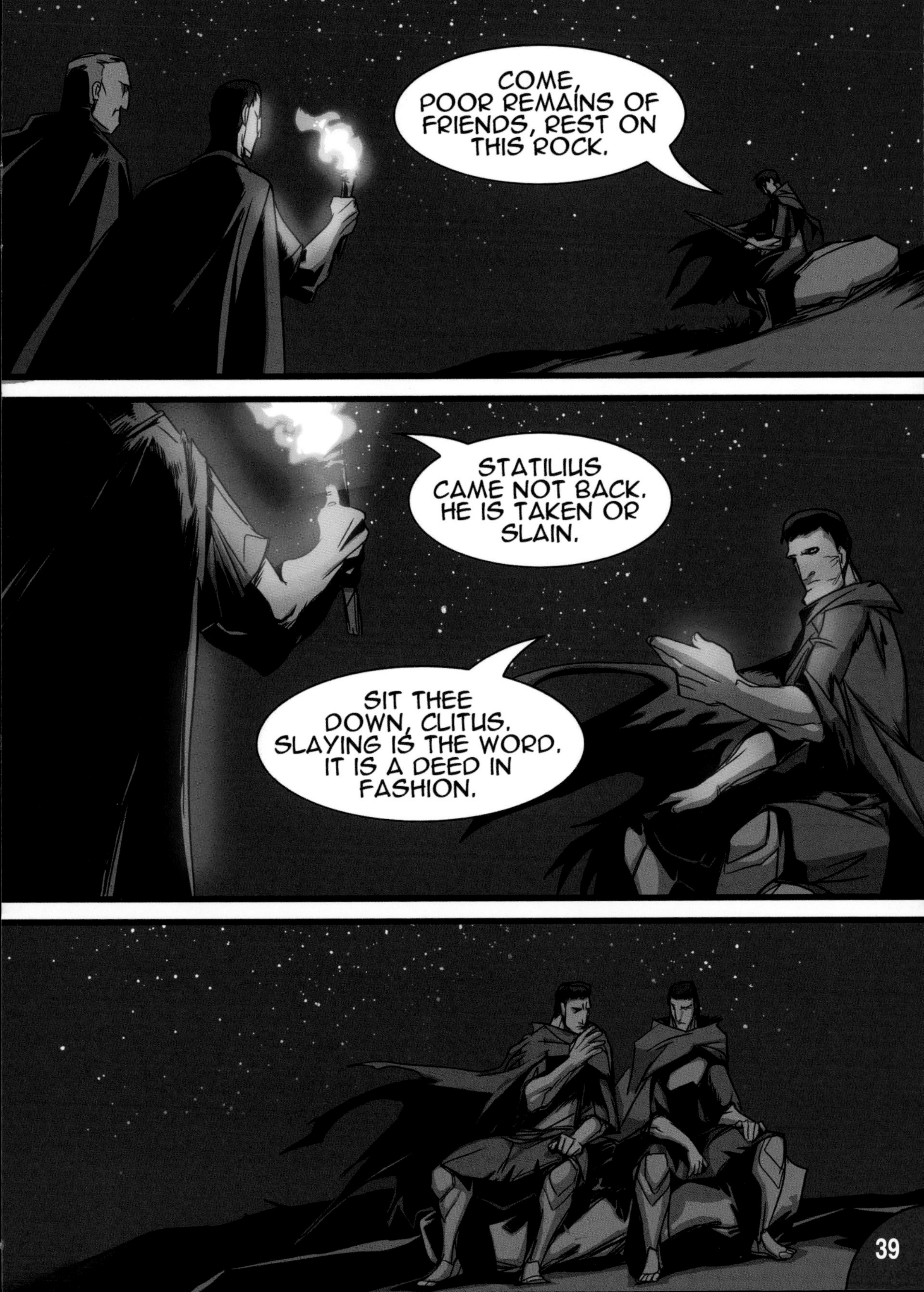
COME, POOR REMAINS OF FRIENDS, REST ON THIS ROCK.
STATILIUS CAME NOT BACK. HE IS TAKEN OR SLAIN.
SIT THEE DOWN, CLITUS. SLAYING IS THE WORD. IT IS A DEED IN FASHION.

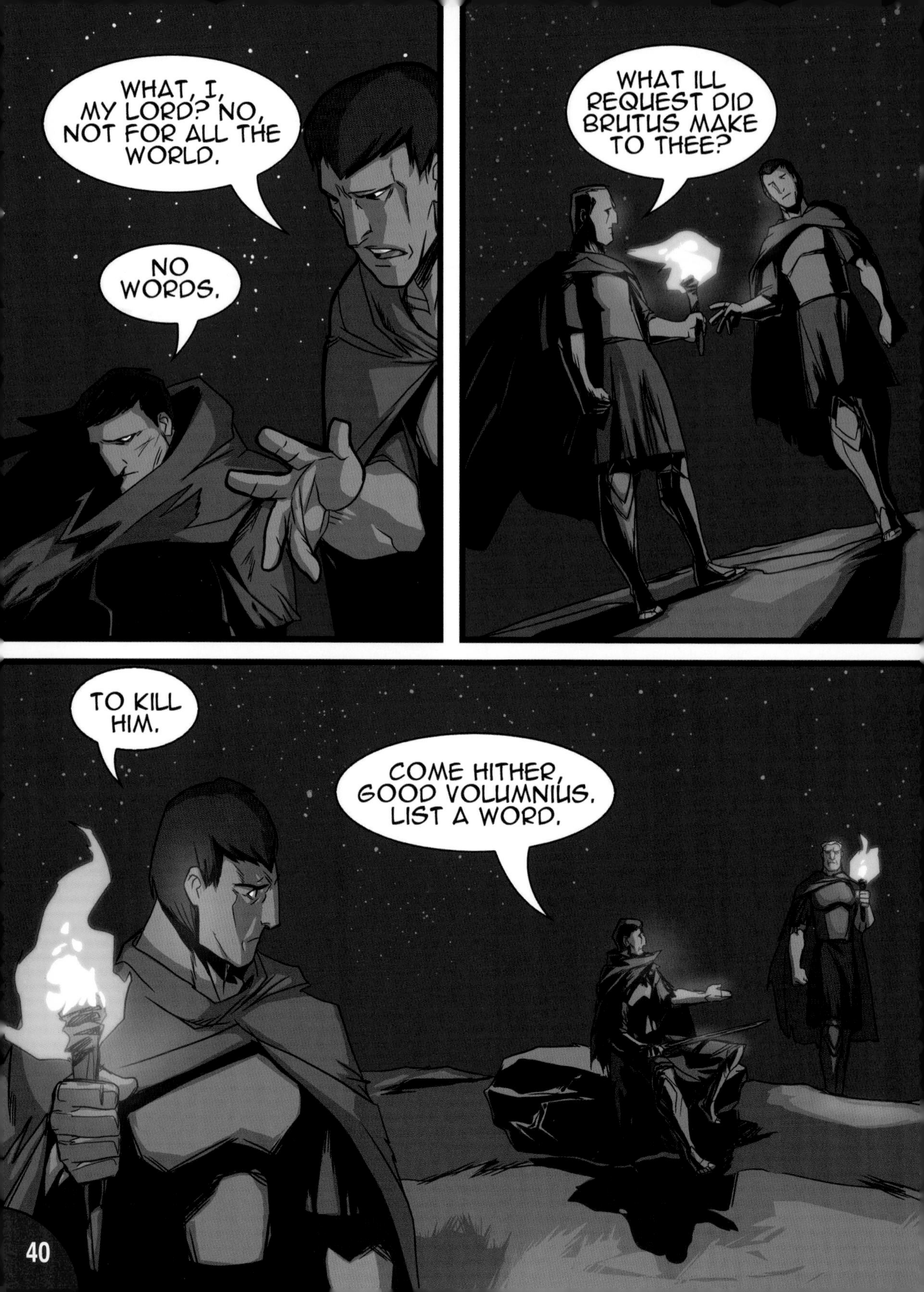
WHAT, I, MY LORD? NO, NOT FOR ALL THE WORLD.
NO WORDS.
WHAT ILL REQUEST DID BRUTUS MAKE TO THEE?
TO KILL HIM.
COME HITHER, GOOD VOLUMNIUS. LIST A WORD.

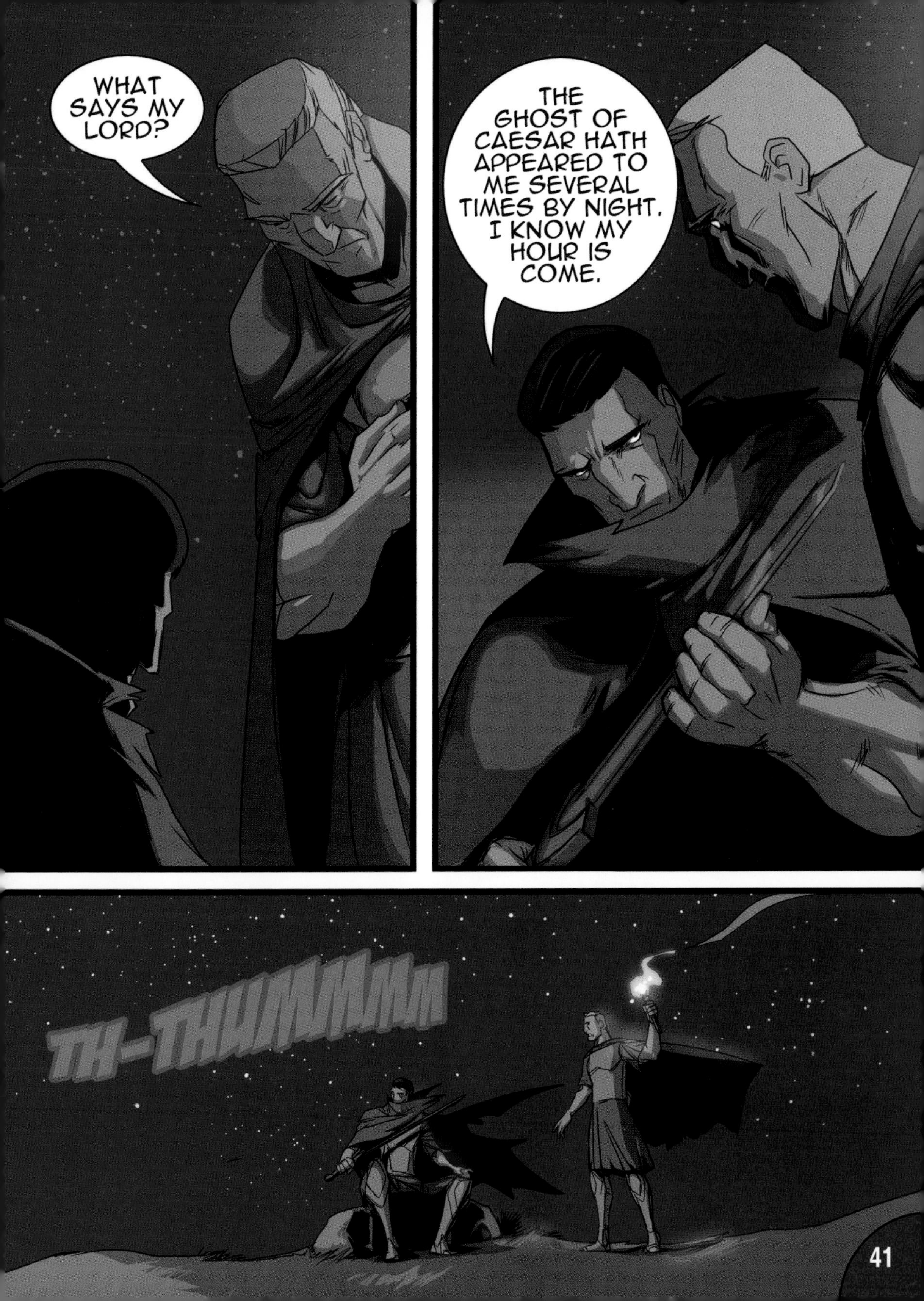
WHAT SAYS MY LORD?
THE GHOST OF CAESAR HATH APPEARED TO ME SEVERAL TIMES BY NIGHT. I KNOW MY HOUR IS COME.
TH-THUMMMM

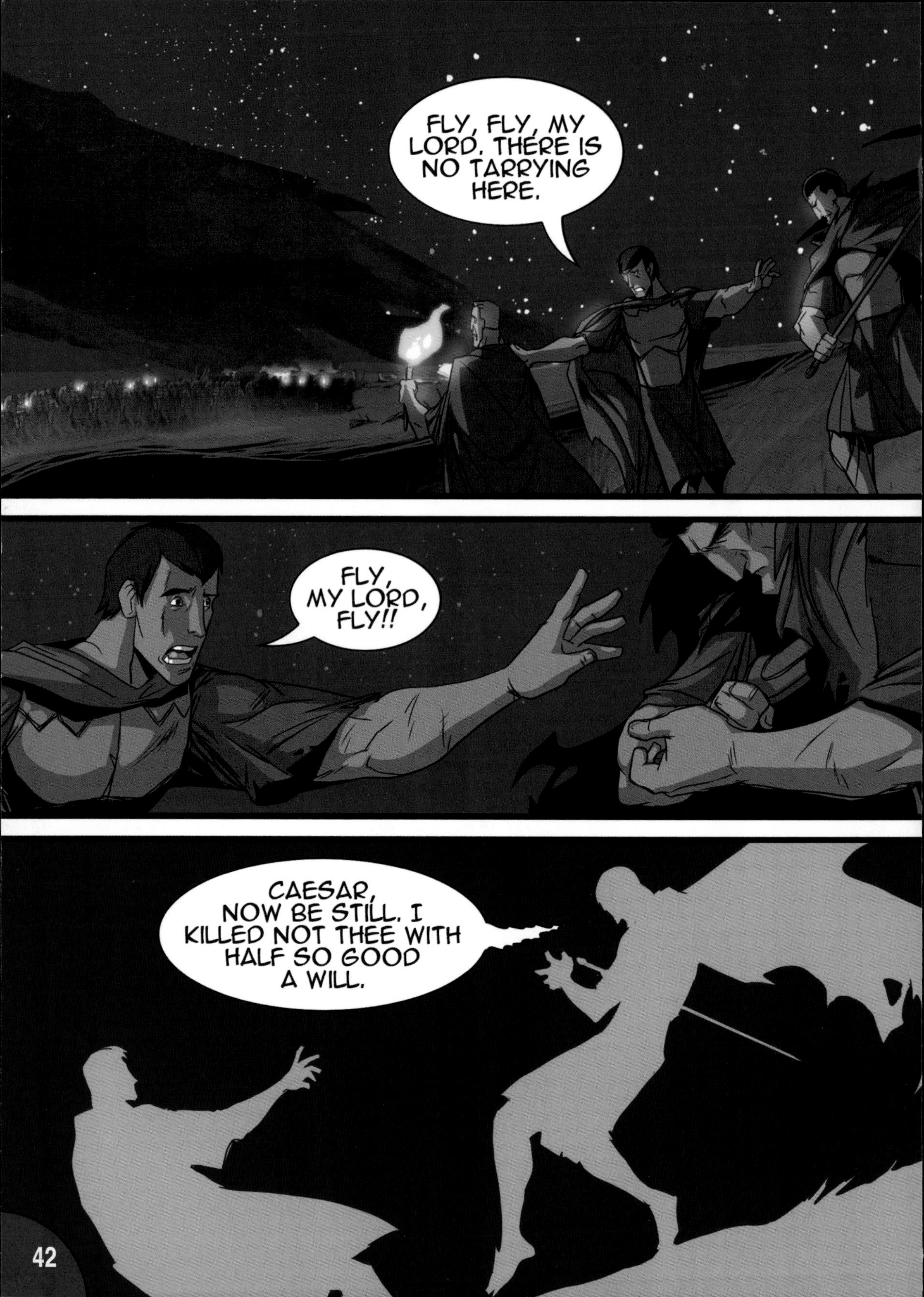
FLY, FLY, MY LORD. THERE IS NO TARRYING HERE.
FLY, MY LORD, FLY!!
CAESAR, NOW BE STILL. I KILLED NOT THEE WITH HALF SO GOOD A WILL.

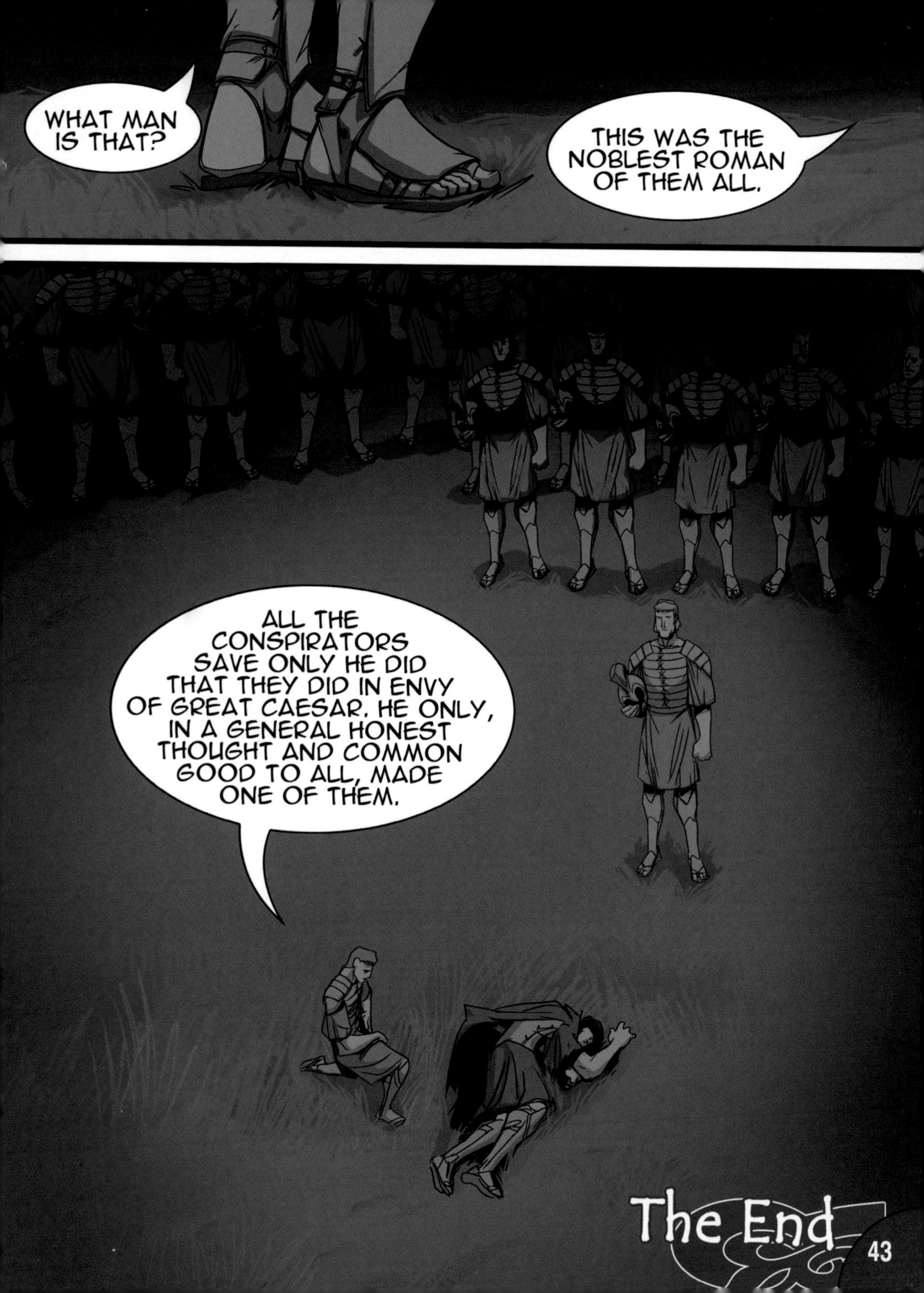
WHAT MAN IS THAT?
THIS WAS THE NOBLEST ROMAN OF THEM ALL.
ALL THE CONSPIRATORS SAVE ONLY HE DID THAT THEY DID IN ENVY OF GREAT CAESAR. HE ONLY, IN A GENERAL HONEST THOUGHT AND COMMON GOOD TO ALL, MADE ONE OF THEM.
The End

Behind Julius Caesar

After Shakespeare had written histories about England, he chose to write about the ancient Romans. He wrote *Julius Caesar* in 1599 to 1600. *Julius Caesar* was the first play he wrote about the Romans.

Julius Caesar was still revered as a great leader in Shakespeare's time. It's not unusual that Shakespeare would have wanted to write about the tragedy of his death.

Shakespeare's plays often focus on human behavior and emotions. *Julius Caesar* is no different. Shakespeare made Caesar's conspirators the focus of the play instead of Caesar.

The play starts with a warning to Caesar about the Ides of March. Cassius and Brutus begin to wonder about Caesar and how the masses love him. If Caesar gained enough respect from the crowds, he would be able to lead by himself. This would wreck the democracy in Rome. Cassius convinces Brutus that it would be the best thing for Rome if Caesar were gone.

Many of the senators get together and kill Caesar. Caesar's friend Antony finds out and is very upset. He asks to speak at Caesar's funeral. At the funeral, he persuades the masses of common people that Caesar was murdered unjustly. He then convinces them that they should kill the men who murdered Caesar.

The play ends in a battlefield near Philippi. There, Cassius and Brutus kill themselves before they have to surrender. Antony is upset that Brutus had to die. Cassius wanted to kill Caesar out of jealousy, but Brutus genuinely thought he was doing the best thing for Rome, which he loved above all.

Julius Caesar is one of Shakespeare's most famous plays. It became popular immediately after it was performed at the Globe Theatre and is still a favorite for audiences. In 1599, Shakespeare became part owner of the Globe Theatre in London, and his plays were performed there. Today, the characters come to life on stages and in films around the world.

Famous Phrases

Et tu, Brute!

Friends, Romans, countrymen, lend me your ears.

I killed not thee with half so good a will.

This was the noblest Roman of them all.

About the Author

William Shakespeare was baptized on April 26, 1564, in Stratford-upon-Avon, England. At the time, records were not kept of births, however, the churches did record baptisms, weddings, and deaths. So, we know approximately when he was born. Traditionally, his birth is celebrated on April 23.

William was the son of John Shakespeare, a tradesman, and Mary Arden. He most likely attended grammar school and learned to read, write, and speak Latin.

Shakespeare did not go on to the university. Instead, he married Anne Hathaway at age 18. They had three children, Susanna, Hamnet, and Judith. Not much is known about Shakespeare's life at this time. By 1592 he had moved to London, and his name began to appear in the literary world.

In 1594, Shakespeare became an important member of Lord Chamberlain's company of players. This group had the best actors and the best theater, the Globe. For the next 20 years, Shakespeare devoted himself to writing. He died on April 23, 1616, but his works have lived on.

Additional Works by Shakespeare

Love's Labour's Lost (1588–97)
The Comedy of Errors (1589–94)
The Taming of the Shrew (1590–94)
Romeo and Juliet (1594–96)
A Midsummer Night's Dream (1595–96)
Much Ado About Nothing (1598–99)
As You Like It (1598–1600)
Hamlet (1599–1601)
Twelfth Night (1600–02)
Othello (1603–04)
King Lear (1605–06)
Macbeth (1606–07)
The Tempest (1611)

About the Adapters

Vincent Goodwin earned his BA in Drama and Communications from Trinity University in San Antonio. He wrote three plays and is the cowriter of the comic book *Pirates vs. Ninjas II*. Goodwin is also an accomplished journalist, having won several awards for his work as a columnist and reporter.

Fred Perry has been working in comics ever since he returned from serving in Operation Desert Storm with the U.S. Marine Corps. He combines a long-standing love of role-playing game campaigns with his expertise in computer programming, marine biology, and military matters to create stories that are intriguing, intense, and fun.

ambition – desire to be powerful or famous.

conspirator – someone who secretly agrees to do an unlawful or wrongful act.

contriver – someone who makes a plan.

mantle – cloak or coat.

misgiving – a feeling of doubt or suspicion for the future.

mutiny – open rebellion against lawful authority, especially by sailors or soldiers against their officers.

reverence – honor or respect.

servile – of or like a slave.

taper – a candle.

tyranny – a government in which one person has absolute power.

Web Sites

To learn more about William Shakespeare, visit ABDO Group online at **www.abdopublishing.com**. Web sites about Shakespeare are featured on our Book Links page. These links are routinely monitored and updated to provide the most current information available.